Gallagher Girls

'I pretty much inhale these books as soon as I get my hands on them and I can't wait for the next! Great fun and totally addictive!' *iwanttoreadthat.com*

'A great guilty pleasure read for those of you out there who also harbour secret dreams of becoming a spy, or even those who just want a light-hearted break … grab a copy, step out of your reality bubble and enjoy' *Teen Today*

'Combines classic teen themes … with a nifty spy hook' *Bookseller*

Embassy Row

'All the nail-biting twists and turns of a spy thriller … will leave readers desperate for the next instalment' *School Librarian*

'Once again Ally Carter has produced a winning plot line … a fast paced and exciting adventure for younger teens' *Books For Keeps*

Heist Society

'Stylish, cool, quick-witted and daring' *Carousel*

'Funny, exciting and intriguing in equal measure, with an original premise, a wicked twist to the plot and a gamut of fascinating characters readers will look forward to meeting again very soon. Don't miss it!' *The Bookbag*

Also by Ally Carter

Gallagher Girls series

1. I'd Tell You I Love You, But Then I'd Have to Kill You
2. Cross My Heart and Hope to Spy
3. Don't Judge a Girl by Her Cover
4. Only the Good Spy Young
5. Out of Sight, Out of Time
6. United We Spy

Heist Society series

1. Heist Society
2. Uncommon Criminals
3. Perfect Scoundrels

Embassy Row series

1. All Fall Down
2. See How They Run
3. Take The Key And Lock Her Up

Not If I
Save You First

For Madeleine Elise Brock,
the original Mad Dog

ORCHARD BOOKS

First published in the United States in 2018
by Scholastic Press

This edition published in 2018 by The Watts Publishing Group

1 3 5 7 9 10 8 6 4 2

A CIP catalogue record for this book is available from the British Library.

ISBN 978 1 40834 909 0

Printed and bound in Great Britain by CPI Group (UK) Ltd, Croydon, CR0 4YY

The paper and board used in this book are
made from wood from responsible sources.

Orchard Books
An imprint of Hachette Children's Group
Part of The Watts Publishing Group Limited
Carmelite House
50 Victoria Embankment
London EC4Y 0DZ
An Hachette UK Company
www.hachette.co.uk

www.hachettechildrens.co.uk

Not If I Save You First

Ally Carter

Chapter 1

SIX YEARS AGO

Dear Maddie,

There's a party at my house tomorrow night. Mom said I can invite a friend if I want to.

So do you want to come?

YES

NO

MAYBE

Logan

Madeleine Rose Manchester had absolutely no intention of invading the White House. But she knew seven different ways she could do it if she'd wanted to.

After all, Logan had lived there less than a year, and already he and Maddie had found four tunnels, two pseudo-secret passageways, and a cabinet near the kitchen that smelled faintly of cheese and only partially blocked an old service elevator that really wasn't as boarded up as everybody thought.

"Charlie?" Maddie asked the big man in the passenger seat of the dark SUV. He turned to look at where she sat, her seatbelt snug around her, even though everyone knew silk wrinkled and Maddie had never had a silk dress before.

She'd already complained about it, but Charlie had told her that it was either wear a seatbelt or walk, and her black leather shoes were new and they'd already started to pinch her feet, and Logan had told her there might be dancing later.

Maddie dearly, dearly hoped there would be dancing …

"Whatcha need, Mad?" Charlie asked while Walter kept driving.

"Did you know there's a place under the stairs in the East Wing that's full of spiders that died during the Nixon administration? Do you think that's true? I don't think that's true," she said without really waiting for Charlie to answer.

"I could ask Dad," Maddie went on. "But he didn't work here then. At least I don't *think* he worked here then. I mean, I know he's old. Like, really, really old. But is he that old?"

Charlie laughed, but Maddie wasn't exactly sure what was so funny. "I'm not sure, Mad, but you should say it exactly like that when you ask him."

This sounded like a very good idea to Maddie. "Thank you, Charlie. I'll do that." She thought for a moment, then went on. "Did you know it's possible to crawl all the way from Logan's dad's office to the press room using the air ducts?"

"No." Charlie shook his head. "It's not."

"Sure it is," Maddie told him. "Logan bet me five dollars that I couldn't do it, so I did it, and then he gave me five ones instead of one five because Lincoln is his favorite."

"You can reach the Oval Office via the air ducts?" Charlie asked, spinning to look at her.

"Yes. But I ruined my favorite pink leggings."

"Then you should definitely tell your dad that."

"He doesn't care about my leggings," Maddie said, and Charlie shook his head.

"Not about that. About ... Never mind, Mad. I'll tell him."

When they finally reached a pair of tall iron gates Maddie couldn't help but swing her legs and nervously kick at the back of Charlie's seat, but Charlie just rolled down his window and told the man with the clipboard, "We have a VIP guest for Rascal."

The guard looked in the back seat and smiled when he saw Maddie. Through the tinted windows she could see other guards circling the vehicle. Dogs sniffed around the bumpers, but the guard kept his gaze trained on her.

"Looks like a high-risk entrant to me, boys. I don't know if we should let her in."

"Hey, Felix," Maddie said, leaning forward. "Did you

know you can fit two kids and three kittens in the little compartment underneath Logan's dad's desk? If the kittens are tame, that is. I wouldn't want to try it with mean kittens."

"Neither would I," Felix said, just as one of the men outside announced, "You're clear!"

Then Felix stepped back and waved them through the gates. "Have fun at the party!"

Logan never had fun at parties. In his experience, they very rarely meant pizza and bouncy castles and ice cream. Not anymore. Sure, there was usually cake. But they were always fancy cakes that were tiny, and Logan's mom usually gave him *The Look* if he ate more than four. And ever since the time he asked the prime minister of Canada if she was going to eat *her* cake he hadn't been allowed to sit at the table with his parents.

Which, in Logan's opinion, was just as well.

"Is Maddie here yet?" he asked his mother.

"I don't know. Is she under the bed?" Logan's mom grinned and glanced through the bathroom door at the giant canopy bed upon which Logan lay.

"No. We don't fit."

"I am not going to ask how you know that," his mother said, then went back to fixing her make-up.

When the phone rang, she reached for it, and Logan

heard her talking.

"Yes? Excellent. Send her up."

"Is Maddie—"

"She's on her way up," his mother told him, and Logan bounded off the bed, ran out into the hallway, then flew down the big stairs of the residence.

The further he got from his mother, the more chaotic everything became. There were people with huge bunches of flowers, and staffers running up and down the stairs in high heels.

But all Logan really saw was Maddie.

"Mad Dog!" Logan screamed from the top of the stairs, racing to join her on the landing below. "You look …"

"Is my dress too wrinkled?" Maddie blurted as if the answer really, really mattered.

He shook his head. "It's … No. I don't think so. It's …"

But Logan trailed off as he followed Maddie's gaze through the bulletproof glass. The chaos of the building all but disappeared as, outside, a helicopter landed on the lawn. A group of men and women were running towards the house, crouching low beneath the helicopter's spinning blades.

Only the last two men off the chopper walked upright, laughing and talking as they strolled towards the doors.

Maddie turned to Logan. "Dad's home."

Maddie couldn't be sure if she was talking about Logan's father or her own. The statement was true in either case. But there was no denying that, as the two dads came into the house, the place went a little more – and a little less – crazy.

There was an energy that always surrounded Logan's father. Some people stopped. Some people stared. But there was another group of people who seemed to constantly swirl and swarm around him, like a hive of bees caught inside a series of very tiny tornadoes, spinning in his orbit while everyone else hurried to get out of the way.

Everyone except Logan's mom. She didn't spin or rush or stare as she walked towards her husband, her red dress flowing behind her as she moved down the stairs.

"You're late," she said.

"Mr President," one of his assistants cut in. "The speaker is waiting for you."

"He can wait until the president has kissed his wife and hugged his son and … changed into something decent," the first lady told the woman. And with that, the tiny tornadoes moved on to another part of the White House.

"Hello, darling," Logan's dad told the first lady as he leaned down to kiss her.

When he pulled away she made a face and said, "You smell." Then she shifted her gaze onto Maddie. "What are we going to do with them, Mad?"

Maddie could only shake her head. "Boys always smell," she said truthfully.

"You get used to it, sweetheart," Logan's mom told her.

But Logan's dad didn't seem to mind. He just reached for his son and said, "Hey, kiddo." Then he turned to Maddie. "Kiddette."

Maddie dropped into a curtsy. "It's a pleasure to see you again, Logan's dad."

"And you, Manchester's daughter." The president bowed at the waist. "You are a far lovelier sight than your father, I can assure you."

"Thank you. My dress wasn't wrinkled when I put it on, you should know. The wrinkles are entirely Charlie's fault."

"I'll have a word with Charlie," the president said as Maddie's dad tried to pull her into a hug.

"Come here, Mad."

She pulled away and looked at the first lady. "You're right. They do stink."

"This is what I get for keeping the president safe?" Maddie's father asked.

"From treasonous deer? It's hard work, I'm sure." The first lady turned to her husband. "Now do I need to remind the pair of you that the Russian prime minister and his entire entourage, your entire cabinet and all seven viewers of C-SPAN are expecting our very first state dinner to commence in forty-five minutes?"

Logan's dad cut a look at Maddie's. "Save me from her, Manchester."

But Maddie's father just shook his head. "Sorry, Mr President. This time you're on your own."

It wasn't until the first lady dragged the president upstairs that Maddie felt Logan stir beside her. He'd been perfectly quiet – perfectly still – as if content to be a mere fly on the wall in the president's presence.

Then her father asked, "How you doing, Rascal?" and Logan's eyes got bigger.

"Did my dad really kill a deer?"

"No." Maddie's father crouched against the windowsill, bringing himself down closer to Logan's level. "Your father and a senator from Kentucky and I sat in a tree in the woods for seven hours, hoping to kill a deer."

"And you didn't see one?" Logan asked.

"No." Maddie's dad shook his head slowly. "We saw one."

Logan's eyes were wide. "And my dad didn't shoot it?"

"No." Maddie's dad sounded like he was carefully considering the answer. "Your dad was more interested in getting a vote out of the senator from Kentucky."

Logan still looked confused. "You had a gun. Why didn't you shoot it?"

Maddie's father seemed to think this was an excellent question. He leaned a little lower. "Because when I shoot, it isn't for fun."

"It's because you have to," Logan said.

Maddie's father nodded. "And what's more important than shooting, Rascal?"

Logan only had to think about the answer for a moment. "Making sure you don't have to?"

Maddie's dad tousled Logan's hair. "Good job."

When Maddie's father tried to pull her into another hug, Maddie pushed him away even though her dress was already wrinkled. "You really do smell, Dad."

"OK, Mad Dog. I give up. I'll go shower." He started down the stairs. "Now what are you two going to do in the next forty-one minutes?"

Maddie and Logan looked at each other and gave almost identical shrugs.

"Fine," her dad said. "Don't tell me. Just stay in the house and stay out of the way. It's kind of crazy around here."

He was almost out of sight before they said in unison, "We noticed."

Maddie was used to being pseudo-invisible, but Logan had been in the spotlight so often in the past year or two that she could tell it was something of a new, but not entirely unwelcome, feeling as they walked through the chaos of the White House.

Doors slammed and phones rang, but no one noticed the first son and his friend, even when Logan said "In here" and punched numbers into a keypad beside a door that Maddie had never noticed before. When the door sprang open, he pulled Maddie into a hallway that was totally and completely silent.

"That's better," he said, then smiled at her.

"Are we supposed to be in here?"

Logan shrugged. "Probably not. But if they really wanted to keep us out, they shouldn't have let me see them punch in the code that one time."

Maddie thought he made a very excellent point. Everyone knew that Logan was really good at remembering things. All the things. Like phone numbers and access numbers and where the White House stored its chocolate.

It had been Maddie's experience that the White House maintained a supply of excellent chocolate. And that's what Maddie was thinking about when they found themselves in a long, empty hallway that ran from the loading docks to the kitchen. They walked in silence for a long time, until they reached a place where the hall branched, and Maddie knew they should turn around. Her dad and Logan's parents were going to be looking for them soon.

She was just about to drag him back to the crowds and the people and the noise when three men came rushing down the corridor, pushing a large rolling cart, almost oblivious to the two ten-year-olds who stood in their way.

Logan said, "Excuse me," because he was a good kid that way.

But Maddie's dad's job didn't depend on her being nice to strangers, so she said "How rude!" as they passed.

For a moment, she and Logan stood together in the corridor, a little bit stunned. Then something about the men and their location within the White House made her stop. Wonder. "Are they supposed to be here?" she asked.

Logan grimaced. "Russian security. The Russian delegation said they would only eat their own food prepared by their own chefs. They had to bring it in and keep it under armed guard and everything."

Maddie made a face. "I wouldn't like that. Eating cold food just because someone might want to kill me."

She was just starting to say something else when, suddenly, Logan reached into his pocket and blurted "Here!" as he thrust a small blue box towards her.

"What is it?" Maddie asked.

"A gift," Logan said. "For you."

"You got me a gift? Why?"

Logan looked like he wanted to roll his eyes, but he didn't. "Because you're my friend."

"Did you get something for all your friends?" she asked him.

Even in the too-bright fluorescent glare of the hallway, a shadow seemed to cross over Logan's face.

"You're my only friend," he said, and Maddie didn't ask any more questions.

She reached for the package slowly. Reverently. Then she pulled on the little white bow and opened the box. A moment later she was looking down at a piece of gold.

"It's so shiny," she said.

"It's a bracelet. Do you like it?"

"I love it."

Logan helped her put it on, and Maddie turned her wrist, letting the light reflect off the delicate chain and dangling charms.

"It's a little big," he told her. "But I wanted you to be able to wear it when you get older."

"I'll never take it off," Maddie said, and in that moment she had never meant anything more.

A silence stretched between them, and Logan had to look away, like staring at Maddie and her shiny gold bracelet was like staring at the sun. He blinked and said, "Well, I suppose we should get—"

"What are you two doing down here?" The first lady's voice echoed down the tiled hall, cutting Logan off.

"We're staying out of the way," Maddie announced as she spun. She was very proud of that fact and thought it was high time some grown-up praised them for their discretion.

"That's a good plan," Logan's mother told her. "It's a zoo out there."

"Mom, do Maddie and I have to go? Couldn't we just watch TV in the residence or something?"

When the first lady looked at Logan her eyes were a little sad, like part of her wished that she could give him a normal night in a normal house. But Logan was never going to be normal ever again, and she couldn't bring herself to lie about it.

"You could watch TV," the first lady told him. "But I'm afraid tonight is very important for your father. Our relations with Russia are … strained. And he thinks that if you and I go, it might be more of a family thing than a political thing. Does that make sense?"

Logan nodded grimly. "Yeah. It does." Then he looked at his mother as if he were seeing her for the first time. "Why are you down here? Were you looking for us?"

"No." She smoothed the part of his hair that never did lie flat. "The kitchen called. There's some sort of problem, though why they need me I'll never know. I like your bracelet, Maddie."

Maddie hid her blush.

"I like your dress."

"Me too. Mainly because it does *this*." When the first lady started to spin, the wisps of red fabric floated around her like a cloud.

"It's a twirling dress!" Maddie wanted to clap.

"I know!" The first lady sounded like a ten-year-old herself.

Logan looked like he would never, ever understand girls, but he didn't bother to say so.

"Well, I'd better go see what they want so we can get this show on the road. You two should head that way. We'll be starting soon."

"Yes, ma'am," Maddie said as the first lady walked away, leaving Maddie and Logan alone.

They'd been alone about a thousand times over the

past year, but when Maddie moved, her bracelet jingled and it felt like a different kind of alone than they had ever been before.

"So ..." Logan said, looking at her.

"So ..." Maddie said back, because what else could she do?

He held his arm out. "Shall we, my lady?"

Maddie dropped into a crooked curtsy, then took his arm. "Why yes, sir."

They didn't talk. They didn't laugh. They just walked towards the fanciest party in the country, arm in arm, like they weren't ten years old at all.

This time, they heard the three men before they saw them. The big cart made a squeaky, rattling noise as it rolled over the tiled floor, and Maddie and Logan knew to move out of the way. Russians, it seemed, liked to take their half out of the middle, so she and Logan pressed against the wall, and Maddie felt the cool tiles through the mesh fabric on the back of her dress.

The men were shouting loud and fast in Russian, and Maddie didn't understand a word. She just pressed close to Logan for reasons she didn't know or understand.

Two of the Russians seemed really young, probably in their twenties. They had short dark hair and expensive suits with ugly ties. One of them pointed to the doors that seemed a mile away and Maddie caught the flash of a tattoo on his wrist – a weird two-headed bird being eaten by a wolf.

Her first thought was that she couldn't imagine why anyone would want something that ugly on their skin forever.

Her second thought was that the muscles in Logan's arm had gone suddenly tight. Her hand hurt as he bent his arm, squeezing her fingers in the bend of his elbow. But Logan didn't even notice.

When the men passed, Maddie felt a rush of air, like a breeze in their wake. But one of the men – the one with the tattoo – paused for just a moment. He looked right at Logan, recognizing him. Considering something. When the other men shouted he kept his eyes trained on Logan.

Then he said something in Russian.

And winked.

But it wasn't playful. It wasn't teasing. And right then Maddie's head knew what her gut had suspected since she first saw their ugly ties: These men weren't Russian secret service. Maddie knew it in her bones, in her blood.

So who were they?

And why were they there?

Suddenly, Maddie's throat was tight; her heart was pounding.

"Logan … " she started, but Maddie trailed off when she followed Logan's gaze.

The Russians were ten feet away and moving fast towards the doors to the loading dock, pushing the heavy cart that seemed heavier than when they'd pushed it in.

If they were bringing in their delegation's meals,

wouldn't the cart be lighter on the way out? Maddie wondered.

And then she saw it: the piece of gauzy red fabric that protruded from beneath the container's door, floating on the breeze.

"Logan?" The word was practically a gasp.

Maddie felt him moving, digging in his pocket as Maddie pulled away. She was starting to run towards them, to chase and follow …

And bite.

Maddie was an excellent biter.

But Logan was grabbing her arm with one hand. In the other, he held the tiny button that he had to keep on him at all times.

He pushed it, and for a second nothing happened. Then Maddie heard her father's voice.

"There you are!" Her dad was smiling, laughing. He was in his dark tux and his hair was still damp from his shower, and he was so handsome and tall and strong. And happy. Her father was happy.

Then he stopped and brought one hand to his earpiece and everything changed.

"What is it?" he asked Logan, who was trembling.

They could still hear the rattling of the cart's wheels as the Russians broke into a run.

"My mom. They have—"

Sirens were starting to blare and Maddie's dad was already breaking away and drawing his weapon. Maddie had seen his gun a million times, but she'd never seen it like that before – like it was an extension of him, a far colder and deadlier limb.

"You two. Hide!" her dad yelled as he started to run.

And the Russians started to fire.

Chapter 2

Maddie knew what her father's job was. In fact, it had been her grandfather's job even before that. Turns out, she came from a long line of people who were made to run *towards* the shots – to step in front of the bullets.

She'd just never really understood why.

But then Logan's mom was in a food cart and her dad was ducking behind a tall stack of water bottles wrapped in plastic, shooting the gun she'd never seen him fire.

It all happened in a second.

And it seemed to take a year.

"Daddy!" Maddie screamed even though she knew not to distract him, to get in the way.

"Maddie!" She felt Logan's hand on her arm. She heard her name screaming from his lips. But her father was still running *towards* the gunmen, and something about that seemed so fundamentally wrong that, for a moment, she could only stand there. Waiting.

All through the White House, sirens screamed.

Logan's panic button had a GPS tracker, so the rest of the Secret Service would be there soon, Maddie knew. They were probably already blocking the exits and barricading the gates.

The president would be halfway to his underground bunker by now. But Maddie was still standing in that corridor, watching her father run. Fire. Fall.

One of the Russians was down. Maddie could see him sprawled at the end of the hallway.

Blood streaked across the floor, and Maddie couldn't help herself.

"Daddy!" she yelled again. She wanted to run to him, but Logan's grip on her arm was too tight.

Her new charm bracelet bit into her wrist as Logan pulled her into a doorway that offered a little cover, but not much. She should have been running, dragging the first son in the opposite direction – towards safety. But Maddie couldn't take her gaze off her father.

He was up again, limping forward and firing more. At the end of the corridor, a door opened. Bright light flooded the hall and there was shouting and running, more agents filing in from that direction.

Behind her, Maddie heard the heavy tread of running feet. The cavalry was coming. The Russians were surrounded.

But an animal is never more dangerous than when it's trapped. One lone Russian remained. For a moment, he was just a dark shape silhouetted against the glare of the bright lights. He stood perfectly still as he raised his gun and leveled it at Maddie's father.

Then the man smiled and, as if pulled by a magnet, the gun moved, to point directly at where Maddie and Logan huddled together.

The man shouted something in Russian – the words echoing off the hard floor and tile-covered walls. Maddie didn't know what he'd said, but she knew what he meant:

That it wasn't over.

That his cause was just.

That, someday, all of civilization was going to know – and fear – his name.

For a second, the world stood still, and then he pulled the trigger just as Maddie's father jumped between the man and Logan.

And fired.

At first the Russian stood, mouth gaping, as if he couldn't quite believe that someone would have the nerve to get in his way. To fire back. To go against whatever master plan had brought him to that place and time.

But then he looked down at his chest, at the place where blood was starting to ooze from beneath his ugly tie, and he dropped to his knees. Then to the floor.

He didn't move again.

"Rascal!" someone shouted, and Maddie could feel the world change as the rest of the Secret Service swarmed around them.

"The first lady!"

Maddie's father's voice sounded faint, like he was half asleep, and yet he was still dragging himself towards the box. Blood trailed behind him, and Maddie couldn't be held back any longer.

She pulled away from Logan just in time to hear Charlie yell, "Maddie, you and Rascal stay right there!"

The agents were everywhere, a virtual wall between Maddie and Logan and the men who lay, not moving, on the floor, and Maddie knew Charlie wasn't keeping the two of them from danger. He was trying to keep them from the blood and the death and the things no ten-year-old should ever see, but Maddie was already crawling through the agents' legs, pushing towards the place where her father lay, too still on the floor.

There was so much blood.

She was going to ruin her dress.

But Maddie didn't care, so she crawled faster. When one of the agents gripped her around the waist and tried to pull her back, she kicked harder.

Two of the agents were pulling the first lady from the big steel box. She was limp and deathly pale, and everything was wrong.

Everything was so, so wrong, and Maddie had to fix it.

"Let me go!" she snapped at the men and women around her. "Let me—"

"Mad Dog?" Logan's voice was behind her, too soft and too faint – and that was why she turned.

"I got something on my tux," he said, looking down at

the red spot that was on his white shirt and spreading quickly. “I promised I wouldn’t get dirty,” he said, then fell hard to the floor.

Chapter 3

FROM THE DESK OF MADELEINE ROSE MANCHESTER

Dear Logan,

This is called a letter. It's like an email but written on paper and sent through the regular mail (like bills). Your mom gave me this paper. Isn't it pretty? It's called stationery, and she said that I should use it to write to you since my dad says we have to leave.

He doesn't ever talk about why we have to leave. But we're going just the same. Maybe it's because ever since he got out of the hospital our phone keeps ringing. I don't think he likes being a celebrity or whatever. The Man Who Saved the First Lady!

Now he just wants to be the Man Who Doesn't Have a Telephone because we're not going to have one. Or a cell phone. Or Internet. Dad says he thinks it's going to be good for me.

I think it's going to be lonely.

But you can write me back, he says! We can write all the time.

So ... will you write me back?

Your (best) friend,
Maddie

ALASKA
SIX YEARS LATER

Turns out, the key to throwing a hatchet isn't in the wrist, like everyone always says. Sure, it's *a little bit* in the wrist. But it's also in the shoulders. And the hips. But, most of all, it's in the head, Madeleine Rose Manchester thought as she dug her second-favorite hatchet from the base of the big tree nearest to their cabin.

She no longer practiced with her favorite hatchet. No. The grip on that one hadn't been good for throwing ever since she'd bedazzled the handle last winter.

Her dad might have been angry at her if he had even noticed that she'd done it. Which he hadn't. For a man whose very survival had once depended upon noticing everything, he'd developed a nasty habit of not noticing anything in the past six years.

Or maybe, Maddie thought, he just no longer noticed her.

She dug the hatchet from the tree and moved back ten paces.

Twenty.

Thirty.

She took a deep breath, filling her lungs with cool, damp air. The shadows were long and the forest was still and Maddie knew that winter was coming fast.

She had wood to haul.

A chainsaw to sharpen.

Someone needed to crawl on the roof and replace a couple of shingles, then reposition the solar panels that had been blown around by that big storm last week.

She also had a mountain of schoolwork she'd have to send with her father the next time he took the plane to Juneau.

Maybe she could get him to bring her thirty or forty more library books. They hadn't gotten much snow for the past year or two, but the sun was going to go behind a cloud soon, and it wouldn't come out again until Easter. When that happened, Maddie wanted to be ready.

Maddie was always ready.

She took a few more steps back, flipped the hatchet in her hand, drew back her arm.

And threw.

When the hatchet hit the tree, its blade had sunk so deep into the wood that most girls couldn't have even pulled it free. But Maddie was never going to be most girls, she remembered as she jerked the hatchet from the tree and thought about maybe trying it from farther away. Maybe with her left hand.

But that was when she heard it – a hum in the distance, a mechanical whirling sound that broke through the stillness. Maddie turned and watched as the small red dot in the big blue sky grew larger and larger.

When the dot touched down in the middle of the lake and floated towards the cabin, Maddie couldn't help but remember another day. Another landing.

Another world.

"Dad's home," she said, but there was nothing but the wilderness to hear her.

"Mad Dog!" Michael Manchester shouted from the plane as soon as he killed the engine.

He was still a big man. Still strong. Even leaner somehow. In DC, Maddie's father had spent hours boxing and running and lifting weights. He'd taught courses on self-defense and used to spar with the president himself, who had once been an Olympic athlete.

But Maddie watched the man who leaped to the dock from the plane that sat on top of the water, bobbing on the rippling waves. He didn't move like that man used to move.

It could have had something to do with her father's bad leg. Many would have credited the shoulder injury or the three surgeries that had followed it.

But Maddie knew it was Alaska that had changed her father. In Maddie's not-so-uneducated opinion, Alaska could change anyone.

"Hey, kiddo! Did it rain while I was gone?"

"Yes, it rained," she told him. "It always rains."

"Good." He put an arm around her shoulder and pulled her tight against him. "I stink."

"I can tell." Maddie tried to pull away, but her father laughed and pulled her tighter.

"If the barrels are full, I'll heat some water and take a bath. How are you, kiddo?"

When they reached the porch of the small cabin, they both paused and pulled off their boots. It was a luxury, being able to do this outside. Soon it would be too cold, and Maddie wanted to keep the mud out of the house for as long as possible.

Even though *house* wasn't really the right word.

She followed her father into a room that held a wood-burning stove and a rickety table with four chairs. There was a shower rod over an open doorway that led to the kitchen, heavy curtains that could make the room private whenever one of them wanted to pull the tub in from the back porch and heat some water on the stove.

In DC, Maddie's bathroom had been entirely hers, with a pink shower curtain and towels so soft that Maddie would never, ever use them for something like drying her hands. Here, she had a tub and a curtain and, if she was lucky, four barrels full of rain and not ice. It was like that other bathroom – that other life – was just a dream.

The main room held an armchair and a couch and three electric lights that worked as long as the sun was shining in summer or the wind was blowing in winter. And Maddie was grateful for the light. Light meant reading. It used to mean writing. But that was a long time ago. Back when Maddie had someone to write to. But Maddie didn't let herself think about that.

"So how are you, kiddo?" her father asked again. He was unloading his backpack, pulling out a few of the supplies he'd promised to bring back.

"Fine," she said.

It took a moment, but her father laughed.

"What is it?" she asked, and he shook his head.

"Nothing. It's just … I guess it finally happened," he said.

"What?"

When her father looked at her again, she couldn't tell if he was happy or sad. "You ran out of words." He started unloading library books, stacking them on their only table. "I knew you'd use them all up eventually, as fast as you went through them when you were a kid."

Maddie didn't know why exactly, but something in that sentiment stung. "I'm still a kid."

"What was that, sweetheart?" he asked, turning to her.

Maddie shook her head. "Nothing."

He looked like a man who knew better than to argue.

He pulled half a dozen newspapers from his backpack and those landed on top of the pile of books. On the cover of one, she saw a headline about the president, some trip he was taking overseas. She wondered briefly if her father was jealous of the men and women who'd be going with him. But, no; if her father had wanted that life, he could have had it.

Maddie was the only one who'd never been given a choice.

In the beginning, she used to ask her father why they'd left DC, when they'd return. At first the answers didn't make any sense. (For example, Maddie seriously doubted that they had to leave because Miss America had fallen in love with her father and wasn't going to rest until she became Maddie's stepmother.)

But then the answers stopped being crazy and started not coming at all, so Maddie didn't bother asking anymore. This was their home. This was their life. And the life that came before was nothing more than a very elaborate dream.

"Do you have any letters for me to take on my next run?" he asked. It was like he could read her mind sometimes, and when that happened Maddie was glad she lived in a small house in a huge forest. If the bears could read her mind, at least they had to keep their thoughts to themselves.

"Do you *bring* me any letters?" she asked.

Her father shook his head.

"Then that's your answer."

Chapter 4

Dear Logan,

Dad said we'd have a house.

Dad LIED.

It's a cabin, he says, but it's more like a shack. I have my own room, though. Well, technically, I have a little loft that he built in the main room. It's just a mattress sitting on a platform and a little lamp. But there's a curtain I can draw if I want privacy, and I have it to myself. At least I do when I'm not sharing it with the local wildlife. (Some people will tell you that squirrels are cute and cuddly. They are not. You can consider yourself warned!)

I'm sorry I can't reply to anything you've said in your letters, but they haven't gotten here yet. They're probably in the mail.

I really hope they're in the mail.

Maddie

ALEXANDRIA, VIRGINIA

Logan couldn't hear the music. It simply pounded, beating in his skull until he wanted to scream. And maybe he would. It's not like anyone would hear it. He highly doubted anyone would care.

With so many bodies pressed so close he was almost anonymous here. Almost. But not quite.

He was a little taller than average, his hair a little darker. Only two percent of the population had green eyes. But Logan's most distinguishing feature was his shadow.

As he pushed through the crowd of bodies on the dance floor he could feel the big man following in his wake. And a little part of Logan wanted to crawl in some hole and hide. At least until the election was over and America had a new president. Maybe he or she would even have a screwup son, if Logan was lucky. But Logan hadn't been lucky in a really long time.

The noise level dropped a decibel or two when he pushed out of the living room and down a hall that led to the kitchen, where the game was already underway.

"Well, if it isn't the first son and his shadow!" Logan's least favorite person said two seconds after he walked through the swinging door.

The light was a little bit brighter in here, the music a

little bit softer. For once, Logan could actually hear himself think.

"You should fold, Dempsey," he said.

"What?" Dempsey asked.

Logan looked down at the table covered with brightly colored chips and overturned cards.

"You should fold," he said again. "You know, quit while you're ahead."

Dempsey looked like he wanted to get out of his chair and fold Logan into a new shape, and he might have tried if not for Logan's shadow.

"What do you know about it?"

Logan didn't miss a beat. "I know you need a queen to make your straight, which means you've got an eight percent chance under the best of circumstances, which this isn't, considering Peterson there is holding one already."

Now Dempsey really did get up. "You cheating or something?"

"No." Logan shook his head. "I'm paying attention."

Logan always paid attention. To everything. Sometimes two inches of bright red fabric was all that stood between life and death, after all. Once you came to grips with that, cards were easy.

The whole table – the whole game – made sense to Logan with one glance. For a second, he wanted to join his friends. And he would have, if he hadn't noticed long ago that they weren't really his friends at all.

The music got louder for one brief moment as the door behind him opened and closed. Logan didn't turn around, though. Charlie had his back. So Logan wasn't expecting it when an arm slid around his neck and a soft cheek pressed against his.

"Logan!" the girl practically screamed. She slurred her words slightly and felt unsteady on her feet as she pulled Logan even closer. Then her phone was in her free hand and she was screaming, "Let's take a selfie!"

A bright flash filled the air and Logan's eyes burned while Charlie yelled, "No phones!"

"But my followers!" the girl complained as Charlie ripped the phone from her hands.

"You'll get this back at the end of the night," Charlie told her. He slid the phone into his pocket and glanced at Logan as he questioned the girl. "How did you get this in here, anyway? We've got agents at the gate. They should have taken your phone."

The girl looked confused. "They did take my phone. That's my backup phone."

Charlie wanted to groan, Logan could tell. "I've got to go talk to someone," Charlie yelled over the still-pulsing music. He stepped towards the door but stopped himself.

"Something wrong?" Logan asked as if he didn't already know exactly what Charlie was thinking. "You can leave me alone for five minutes, you know."

"That's what you said in Paris."

"I apologized for Paris," Logan reminded him. "And Berlin. But I refuse to apologize for London because those scones I brought you were delicious."

"*Rascal*." Charlie sounded like a man who couldn't decide whether to laugh or cry or just shake the boy he was paid to protect.

"What? Are you afraid I'm going to sneak out and go to a wild party? Charlie, I'm at a wild party. Besides, I need to go to the bathroom. Or are you going to follow me in there, too?"

"It was discussed after Buenos Aires."

At this, Logan shook his head. "Yeah. Well. We all have things we regret about Buenos Aires."

Logan eased closer to the bathroom, and Charlie eased towards the door.

"Charlie, go! Yell at the new guys."

"You've got your panic button?" Now Charlie sounded like a little old lady and not a former Navy SEAL.

"Of course," Logan said. It was the one Secret Service rule he never, ever broke. That button had saved his mother's life, and Charlie must have known it because he turned and pushed his way back through the crowded house.

He was gone before Logan did, in fact, go to the bathroom, where he removed two items from his pocket.

One was a small transmitter with state-of-the-art GPS and a button that, when pushed, could bring forth the hounds of war.

Another was a hot-pink cell phone with a not-too-terrible picture of a pretty girl and the president's son. Logan didn't stop to wonder how long it would take Charlie to realize Logan had picked his pocket. He just posted the picture to her account. The girl had followers to consider, after all.

Then he placed the panic button on the bathroom vanity, right where Charlie wouldn't have to look for it. Just because it was a rule he'd never broken before didn't mean there wasn't a first time for everything.

As he walked to the back door and across the dark, deep lawn, Logan never once looked back.

It was ten minutes before Charlie realized that he was no longer in the bathroom.

"Eight hours. You were gone for eight hours! *What were you thinking?*"

The Oval Office was one of the most intimidating rooms in the world – at least that's what the White House tour guides liked to say. But even though the room was powerful, Logan had figured out long ago that it had nothing on the man.

The president's jacket was draped over the back of his chair and his shirtsleeves were rolled up, his red power tie loosened. It was his working-man-stump-speech look – the one that went over well in midwestern mill towns. But in the Oval, it made him look like a man who had immense power at his disposal but would rather tear a person in two with his bare hands than bother calling in the marines.

"*Were* you thinking?" the president yelled again, and Logan forced a shrug.

"It wasn't a big deal."

"I'll tell you when it's a big deal and when it's not. That's my right as long as I'm—"

"President?" Logan guessed.

"Your father," the president finished.

"News flash: You already got reelected," Logan told him. "Unless you want to be Queen of England or something, you've run your last campaign."

"This isn't about my presidency—"

"I think the Secret Service would disagree," Logan cut in, but his father never slowed down.

"—this is about our family!"

Only then did Logan let himself glance at his mother, who muttered, "Joseph." His father spun on her.

"He posted a picture online and then took a walk. For eight hours. No detail. No panic button. Do you know what could have happened to him?"

"Yes, Joseph." Her voice was soft but strong. Her whisper echoed through the room like a roar. "*I know.*"

They didn't talk about That Day. Not ever. Not in ages. But it was always there, simmering underneath the surface. In many ways, it was his father's legacy: the thing his two terms in office would be remembered for the most.

He was the president who had almost had his wife snatched out from under his nose.

His was the White House with blood on the floors.

"I'm sorry, sweetheart. I forgot," Logan's father said, but that was a lie. He didn't forget. None of them did. Maybe that's why the president spun on Logan and snapped, "Secret Service protocols exist for a reason. You of all people should know that."

"It was a selfie!" Logan couldn't help but shout. "If that were illegal, then every kid in America would be locked up."

"It wasn't just a selfie, and you know it! It was a beacon, transmitting your location to everyone in the world with a cell phone – a location from which you decided to wander off, unprotected. And you aren't just another kid in America. You are the president's son."

"Yeah." Logan bristled. "That's what they tell me."

Something in Logan's tone seemed to break through his father's armor; his rage began to fade into something closer to regret.

"I know you didn't choose this life. I know no teenager in their right mind ever would. But it *is* our life, and when I think about what could have happened … We all *know* what could happen!"

"But it didn't happen!"

As soon as the words left Logan's mouth, he knew he was going to lose. Worse, he knew he should.

He was being stupid. He was being careless. He was

being selfish and stubborn and almost too clichéd for words. But he hadn't been able to help himself. Not in London or Berlin or Buenos Aires. Logan really was his own worst enemy, which was saying something, he knew.

"I'll apologize to Charlie. I won't do it again."

"Oh, I know you won't do it again. But it's too late to apologize to Charlie."

"What do you mean?"

"I mean Charlie got hoodwinked by a sixteen-year-old. Again. So Charlie doesn't work here anymore."

"What? Did you transfer him to Treasury or—"

"Charlie has a nasty habit of losing the president's son, so now Charlie's got to find a new job."

"You can't do that!" Logan snapped. But the president smiled.

"I can do anything. I'm not just the president of the United States. I'm *your father*."

"Joseph," the first lady warned.

"Come on, Dad. You've got, what? A year left in office? What are you going to do, lock me up until CNN stops caring about us?"

For a moment, Logan's parents seemed to consider the idea, but then a smile passed between them. Which was worse.

"If the Secret Service can't keep you offline and out of trouble, then we're going to send you someplace where online and in trouble isn't an option."

Logan didn't even try to bite back his laugh. "Yeah,

Mr President. Good luck finding that."

Logan was already to the door, his hand on the knob, when his mother said, "Oh, we've already found it."

Chapter 5

Dear Logan,

We've been here six months already. I can't believe it. Can you believe it? It feels like we just got here. And in other ways, it feels like I've never lived anywhere else. Like my old life was just a dream.

Were you a dream?

I told Dad that this has been a most excellent experience, but I'm ready to go back to our real life now.

He just smiled and said this is our real life. I asked him when we were going back and he didn't answer. Which is an answer all its own, isn't it?

Sometimes I think he doesn't want to go back. And sometimes I think he can't. We can't.

I just don't know why.

Maddie

"Come here, kiddo. There's something we need to talk about."

The last time Maddie's dad had said those words she'd found herself on three planes (each progressively smaller than the last) within a week. So, needless to say, she wasn't the good kind of excited as he pulled up a chair at their old, battered table.

Maddie had never really understood why they had four chairs. It's not like they did a lot of entertaining. Not unless you counted the time Maddie had forgotten to lock up her cereal in an airtight container and a bear had tried to break through the cabin's front door. Which Maddie totally did not count. That bear hadn't been invited and would never be welcome again.

So she didn't really trust the look in her dad's eyes when he glanced at the empty chair that wasn't stacked high with library books.

"Where are you going this time?" she asked because she knew him well. Too well.

It had been just the two of them since Maddie was three and her mom had died. And that was before they'd moved to the middle of nowhere. For six years it had been just the two of them. If Maddie didn't know her father, she didn't know anyone. There were no other options.

"I'm not going anywhere," he said quickly. Guiltily. "Or, well, I'm not going right now."

"Then what is it?" It took a lot to scare Madeleine Rose

Manchester. She'd seen her father take a bullet. When she got up to pee in the middle of the night she usually carried a revolver. Fear and Maddie went way, way back, but she'd never seen her father look quite like he looked then.

"Nothing's wrong, kiddo. It's just that … I'm expecting … I mean … I heard from DC."

That, at last, stopped Maddie's heart from racing. At that point, Maddie's heart wasn't beating at all.

Maddie thought her father had burned that bridge, salted the earth, gone as far off the edge of the map as possible, and then dropped straight down and landed here, smack dab in the middle of nowhere.

"You're not going back," Maddie blurted because, it turned out, there *was* something worse than moving to a place where your best friends were either fictional or fur-covered. There was knowing your dad might take *another* bullet. "You quit," she reminded him.

"That's right, kiddo. I did quit. And they wouldn't have me anyway, even if I wanted to go back. Remember." He patted the leg that still ached sometimes and pulled aside the collar of his shirt just far enough for her to see his second-biggest scar.

"Yeah." Maddie laughed. But it wasn't funny. "Kind of hard to forget."

"I'm sorry, kiddo. What I'm trying to say is … the president and the first lady are sending us a surprise."

For a moment, Maddie couldn't help herself. She

thought about the ice-cream sundaes that the White House chef used to make. She remembered one time when the first lady let her try on the shoes she'd worn to the inaugural ball. She could almost smell the new leather of her favorite chair in the White House screening room.

So when her dad got up and walked to the door she wasn't really following him, not consciously. She just couldn't stay behind.

Maddie could never stay behind.

"What's the surprise?"

As soon as they stepped off the porch, Maddie felt it. Or maybe she saw it. Heard it? She couldn't be sure. She just knew that something big was coming. Ripples spread across the water of the lake, and the trees started to toss and sway.

Glacier silt lined the banks of the lake, and it swirled like sand, stinging and blinding. A part of Maddie knew what she was going to see long before the helicopter appeared, hovering over the trees and then dropping softly to the ground.

"What kind of surprise, Dad?" Maddie asked again as his arm went around her, pulling her tight. Maybe she knew the answer. And that's why she pulled back, why she squeezed her eyes shut. It had nothing to do with the wind that swirled around her, full of silt and gravel and leaves.

Maddie knew that as soon as she opened her eyes, she was going to see a ghost.

But it turned out she didn't have to see him to know him. She just had to hear the words, "Hey, Mad Dog."

It's really her.

Logan shook his head for a moment. He couldn't be sure if he'd said the words out loud or not. Probably not. He glanced up at Mr Manchester, studied his face. Definitely not. Maddie and her father weren't looking at him like he was stupid. They were looking at him like he was different.

And he was.

Some guys hit puberty and turn into football players or wrestlers or big, hairy creatures who look like science-lab experiments or something. Logan had just … grown. Everywhere. It felt like his fingers were a foot long. His feet seemed always at risk of bursting out of his shoes. His pants and his shirts, too. He was like the Incredible Hulk except not green and not quite so angry.

Oh, he was definitely angry. But he could also feel it fading a little. Like he was still in the helicopter, looking down on the lake and about a million acres of wilderness and the tiny dot that was his destination. Logan's anger looked smaller from there, like it was a long way off. And now there was only him and Mr Manchester and a girl he used to know.

"It's you."

This time he definitely said it aloud because Maddie's dad glanced at her, then held out his hand for Logan.

"Good to see you, Rascal."

Mr Manchester shook his hand like he was a man, but something about it made Logan feel more like a kid than ever. He'd been through probably twelve pairs of sneakers since he'd last seen the man, but in Mr Manchester's presence Logan felt as if he might be ten until the end of time.

"You, too, sir," Logan said. He watched Maddie listen to the words. She didn't say a thing.

"How are your parents, Logan?" It was the first time Mr Manchester had ever called him by his first name. It made Logan pull back for a moment, rethink things. Remember that Maddie's dad wasn't the head of the president's detail anymore. Now he was just Logan's dad's friend. And this wasn't supposed to be fun.

"My parents are well, sir. The president's blood pressure was a little high the last time I saw him, but that's to be expected."

"Yes. I imagine it is," Mr Manchester said, then smiled.

"Is that why they're punishing you?" Maddie asked. "I mean they are punishing you, right? Why else would anyone come here?"

Logan watched her speak. Her voice was the same, but her mouth was different. Why had Logan never noticed her mouth before? Her bottom lip was fuller, but the top lip was shaped like a little bow, and he couldn't decide which lip he liked more. He knew he was going to have to do a lot more looking in order to choose. And it suddenly felt imperative that Logan choose very, very well.

He was aware, faintly, of Mr Manchester shifting, saying "Maddie" like it was some kind of warning. "Logan's parents just asked if he could come here for a bit," her dad finished.

Logan wondered how much Maddie's dad knew. It was clear Maddie knew nothing. Not about Logan repeatedly slipping his detail or Charlie getting fired. Not about the poker club he'd been busted for running out of the Lincoln Bedroom last February, or how he'd gotten really good at forging his father's signature and had sold ten thousand dollars' worth of stuff on eBay before someone at the State Department figured out what he was doing and shut him down.

Logan had started six different social media accounts in the names of former presidential pets, and three were still operational. But if the sixteen followers of @SocksTheCat were wondering why Socks suddenly had so many ... well ... socks (and jackets, and an old copy of *The Call of the Wild*) no one was saying so.

No. Maddie didn't know about any of that. Maddie only knew that they used to be friends, and she looked like maybe that was a decision she might have come to regret.

Logan turned back to Mr Manchester. "I'm glad to see you looking so well, sir."

Maddie's dad laughed and slapped him on the back. "Rumors of my death have been greatly exaggerated."

Logan smiled, but Maddie's voice was cold. "That's not funny."

And Logan remembered.

Blood. Cold tile and the way the shots were quieter than they should have been, and yet the sound seemed to reverberate forever.

"Mad, it's OK," her dad said, but Logan got the feeling that it wasn't – that it really wasn't OK at all.

"How have you been, Mad Dog?" Logan asked, but Maddie just glared at him.

"Awesome!" she said, but Logan was 98 percent certain she was being facetious. It quickly became 100 percent when Mr Manchester said "*Mad*" and she spun on him.

"I'd ask if I could go to my room, but I don't have one."

Then she turned and headed towards the house.

But it wasn't a house. Not really. From where they stood, Logan could see a wooden porch and a steep roof over rough wooden walls made from logs that looked as big around as boulders.

Mr Manchester's hand was firm as it landed on Logan's back. "Come on in. Let's get you settled."

Another helicopter was dropping to the ground just then and silt and gravel whirled, spinning in the air. Mr Manchester had to shout over the noise.

"You go on!" Two agents were hopping out of the helicopter. "I'll get these guys set up."

Mr Manchester shoved Logan's bags into his arms and pushed him towards the cabin. And Maddie.

Logan could hear men shouting. A crew was already unloading huge crates, and someone was setting up a tent. Soon there'd be cameras in the trees and a secure satellite signal trained on this location. But only two agents were staying behind. Logan's dad had been adamant about that.

There would be no chef. No housekeeper. No butler or driver or even someone to wash his sheets. Logan wasn't on vacation. He would have a two-agent detail because that was the minimum, but other than that, his parents would have been just as happy to drop him off in the middle of nowhere and forget about him until the country had a new president.

A pair of small boots sat beside the door of the cabin, so Logan stopped on the porch and took his off as well. When he knocked, the door swung open, and he couldn't help but ease inside.

Logan wasn't really sure what he'd expected. Maybe a moose's head over a roaring fire, a bear-skin rug and steaming mugs of hot chocolate. But it wasn't like that.

There was something like a kitchen in what could have been a small hallway, with a curtain on a rod. Instead of a fireplace, he saw a black stove with a big pile of wood stacked not far away. There were shelves covered with books. A few small, dirty windows and floor lamps provided the only light. There were two doors. Through one, he saw a bed and a dresser. The other went out the back through the kitchen.

"It's not much, but it's home."

Maddie didn't sound ashamed. She just sounded … different. Angrier and more serious somehow. She was supposed to be rolling her eyes at him, teasing him about how big he'd gotten or how silly he was to have come all the way to Alaska and not have brought her a single piece of official White House chocolate.

Maddie was supposed to be smiling. But the girl in front of him looked like maybe she couldn't quite remember how.

"Where's your room?" he asked because he had no idea what else to say.

"Above you."

That's when Logan saw the little ladder beside the door, the loft that sat above the main room, a bright quilt over a small bed.

"That's cool," he said.

"Whatever."

"No. I mean it," Logan said. He'd been living at the most famous house in the world for seven years, and in its own way this small cabin was nicer and happier than 1600 Pennsylvania Avenue would ever be. "This is nice, Mad Dog. It's … warm."

"That's because Mad's got a good fire going!"

Only then did Logan realize they were no longer

alone. Her father was pulling a stack of books from one of the chairs at the table. When Logan turned, he saw a cabinet with sparkly dresses that were two sizes too small for the girl he'd just met. There were old copies of teen magazines and a bottle of fingernail polish by the window. Right beside a hatchet that appeared to have sequins and rhinestones all around the handle.

"*Maddie*." Logan practically exhaled the word, finally seeing something of the girl he used to know in the angry young woman with the utterly fascinating mouth.

"What?" she asked.

"I—"

Logan knew he was supposed to say something. Pay her a compliment. Maybe grovel. His father always said that women expected a great deal of groveling, but Logan didn't know what to say. And, luckily, at that moment a totally different noise filled the air.

Ringing.

When you live in the White House, your whole world is one nonstop chorus of ringing phones, but something about the sound didn't belong in that small cabin.

There were no power lines. No phone lines. No water lines or gas lines. Maddie's world was pretty much line-free. Confused, Logan stole a glance at his best friend, but she wouldn't look at him.

Which meant she probably wasn't his best friend anymore.

The phone rang again, and all Logan could do

was watch as something passed between Maddie and her father, a don't-pretend-you're-capable-of-ignoring-that look.

"I'll call them back," Mr Manchester said. "Now, Logan. Are you hungry? I make a pretty mean pot of chili and Maddie's got some—"

"Base to Ridge Center. Ridge Center, do you read? Ridge Center, this is Base." The voice that filled the air was scratchy, and it took Logan a moment to see the old-fashioned radio that sat on a cluttered desk. "Ridge Center, do you read me?"

"Go ahead," Maddie told her father. "It must be important."

"Sorry, guys," Maddie's dad said as he sat on an old metal office chair and spun, reached for the microphone and answered. "Hello, Base, you've got Ridge Center. Go."

"Hey … Center. We've got a storm … in." The woman's words were spiked with static, coming in fits and starts.

Maddie's dad just laughed a little and pressed the button on the microphone. "It's Alaska, Base. Storms are always moving in."

It took a moment for the woman to answer. "This one's not so normal."

Maybe it was the tone of the woman's voice or the eerie, crackling static that filled the cabin, but Logan thought he could actually feel the air change when

Maddie's father looked back at his daughter.

He pressed the button on the microphone. "How not normal?"

After a beat the woman answered, "We need you to … a run tomorrow morning before … hits."

Logan watched Maddie's face. It wasn't disappointment. She didn't roll her eyes. But it was like a string ran between her and her father, something pulled too tight for too long. He was afraid that it might snap.

"No can do, Base," her dad said. "I just got home."

Home. This place in the middle of nowhere, this building that was something between a cabin and a shack. This was home. And Logan wondered if Maddie felt the same.

"I'm sorry, Mike. I wouldn't ask if … emergency. We've got a group of scientists that were supposed to … resupplied in three days, but if this thing is half as bad as … won't make it then, and … needs medication. This thing might be bad enough that we can't make it in after, and—"

"I read you, Base." Maddie's dad's gaze never left his daughter's. "I'll leave at first light."

Logan heard a door close, but more than anything he felt Maddie's absence. In a way, he realized, he'd been feeling it for years.

"I'm sorry," Logan said, and he meant it. He really did. He was sorry that he'd ditched Charlie. Sorry Charlie had been fired. Sorry that he'd come here and upset whatever fragile ecosystem Maddie and her father had made for themselves.

But most of all Logan was sorry that Maddie no longer smiled when she looked at him. He was sorry that the girl he used to know was gone.

Chapter 6

Dear Logan,

I haven't been eaten by a bear yet. That's the good news. But I think a bear might have eaten your letters.

That's the bad.

Maddie

Maddie didn't turn the light on. Maybe because days were always short in winter, and even though she knew the solar panels would still get some sun and the wind never would stop blowing, she didn't want to drain their batteries just the same. Maybe it was because she knew she should be trying to sleep because at least eight hours was absolutely essential for good skin and clear eyes. All the beauty magazines said so.

Or maybe Maddie just didn't want anyone to see the light that she would shine beneath the curtain of her "room."

That's why she lay, unmoving, for what felt like hours

in the little nest her father had built during their first winter in Alaska. It was always warmer up where she slept, and safe away from any animals that might come calling in the middle of the night. But Maddie liked it mostly because she could pull the curtain and have some privacy, even if it was the kind of privacy one couldn't stand in fully upright and enjoy.

But that night Maddie stayed perfectly still, staring through the darkness until she couldn't take it anymore. Then she couldn't stop herself from reaching down between the mattress and the wall and wiggling her fingers until she found it.

The picture was folded into quarters, and thick lines creased the image. She knew each and every inch of it by heart ... and still she reached for her emergency flashlight, risked a little light in order to look at it again.

Maddie still had that dress. Or parts of it. Their second winter in Alaska, Maddie had read every book the Juneau library had on learning how to sew, and over the years she'd turned all of her old clothes into new clothes. She'd saved the shiny white dress with the silver sequined sash for last. Now it was a jacket that might still fit, but Maddie had never, ever worn it except when she wanted to feel pretty sometimes in the darkest parts of winter.

It was hard to believe that it had once been such a pretty dress. Or that she'd been that happy girl. She wanted to believe that she'd forgotten Logan's face, but she hadn't. She knew him as soon as she saw him. Even though he now looked like a version of Logan that had been stretched and pulled and maybe dosed with some kind of magic potion to make him approximately three times his original size.

But in the picture – in her mind – they were the same height, and he had deep dimples and a mischievous grin and he kept his arm around her, the two of them ready for whatever adventures lay ahead.

As long as they could face them together.

Maddie's cheeks were wet then, and she reminded herself for the millionth time that she was never going to cry over Logan. Never, ever again. Then she took the photo and held it at the creases. It was time, she knew – time to tear it right down the center, rip it into a million pieces and throw them on the fire.

But she slipped it back between the wall and the mattress instead, back where it wouldn't hurt her anymore.

She closed her eyes and rolled over in her bed. She was going to sleep, she told herself. And when she woke up, maybe it would all just be a dream.

But that's when Maddie heard it.

There's a certain kind of noise that people make when they're trying not to make any noise at all, and right then the cabin was full of it.

Feet scraping and banging against chair legs, cabinet doors opening and closing in the dark. Maddie eased down her ladder and flipped on the floor lamp by the desk, but her father didn't whirl. He wasn't surprised. He'd made a career out of never, ever being surprised.

"How's the weather?" Maddie asked.

Her father shook the match in his hand, forcing it out, and Maddie saw the kindling in the stove catch. Soon the cabin would be filled with the smell of wood smoke and coffee.

"It's holding," her dad said with a glance out the window, as if it might have changed in the twenty seconds since he'd last looked. "Go back to bed, Mad."

It wasn't that early. Days are just short in Alaska at the beginning of winter. And the truth was, Maddie was the kind of tired that sleep couldn't really fix.

"When will you be back?" she asked.

"Tonight. If the weather holds."

She heard what he wasn't saying – that this was a big storm. It had to be to scare people who had lived in extreme weather most of their lives. But she also knew that nothing would keep her father from her. Absolutely nothing. And sometimes that was the scariest thing of all.

"I'm OK," she said. "I'll be OK. So don't take any chances. Please. If it's bad, don't risk it. I'll be fine. Don't worry about me."

"Sounds like you're the one who's worried."

"You're about to fly a plane the size of a large car over mountains and glaciers and through what might possibly be the storm of the year. *In Alaska*. So I'm allowed some trepidation."

"Well, I'm leaving my teenage daughter alone with a boy, so I'm allowed some, too."

Maddie couldn't help it – she glanced at the closed door to her father's room. Logan was in there on a small camp bed the Secret Service guys must have brought with them when they set up their little base camp near the trees.

Logan.

"You going to be OK without me?" her father asked. Maddie forced herself to look away from the door.

"It's been six years, Dad. If I weren't OK without you here, I'd be dead by now."

"That's not what I mean, Mad. And I think you know it."

Maddie turned away from the door and the boy who had turned away from her. "Whatever."

"Mad—"

"I'm not going to kill the president's son." *No matter how much I might want to*, she silently added.

"That's not what I'm asking." Her father eased a little closer. Outside, the sun was coming up, and the cabin was the color of glowing coals. "Are you *OK*?" he tried again.

"I'm fine."

Her father filled a thermos with coffee, took it to his pack, then added his satellite phone and his wallet. "I thought you'd be happier to see him. You two were always so close."

"Yeah." Maddie filled a cup of coffee. "We *were*."

The cabin was bright enough that her father could see her face, read her eyes.

"Maybe I shouldn't go."

"No. You have to go. You know you do. We're fine."

"There are two agents in the tents outside. They're in charge of security, but Logan … Logan's supposed to be roughing it."

"Oh, I'm sure he's in the lap of luxury."

"I mean it, Maddie. Make him haul wood. And tote water. And clean fish and fix the roof and whatever else you were going to do. His parents want him to carry his weight. I didn't mean to put this on you but …"

"I'm OK," she said. "We'll be OK."

"If you're sure," her dad said.

Maddie forced a smile. "Of course."

How many times had Maddie watched her father fly away? Too many to count, that was for sure. In the beginning, he took her with him. Her first taste of Alaska came at six thousand feet, soaring over glaciers, skirting above mountains, touching down on lakes so clear and cold that you could practically skip across them on bits of glacier ice, live like the seals that lay sunning themselves on the cold, wet land.

And then Maddie got older and was allowed to stay on

her own for an hour. A day. A night. Her father was never, ever gone more than forty-eight hours, though. That was a rule that neither of them ever said aloud. He'd also never left her *Not Alone* before. And Maddie wasn't at all sure how to take it.

She crept to the closed door of her father's room. There was no light. No movement. It was almost like it was empty, just like always. But it wasn't, and that was a fact that Maddie could never, ever let herself forget.

She started the day's work by drawing the curtain over the kitchen door and heating the water. If the storm was bad, then this might be her last chance for a while, and she felt like she needed her armor for what was coming.

To Maddie, armor meant nail polish. And lip gloss. Really, lip gloss was essential to a girl's self-defense, she was certain. And clean hair. Oh, have mercy, did she ever need clean hair.

She worked as quickly and quietly as she could, and soon she was sinking into a tub full of hot sudsy bubbles, leaning her head back and letting the warm water wash over her.

She was never really warm in Alaska. Sure, sometimes she was hot. And sometimes she was freezing. But a nice, comfortable warm was something she only found in the bath, and so Maddie let herself close her eyes and sink lower and ...

"Hey, Mad. I— Sorry!" The voice came from behind her, and Maddie found herself bolting upright and then sliding down beneath a thick blanket of bubbles.

She hadn't really fallen asleep. She'd just entered into a kind of *it's-early-and-I'm-still-sleepy-and-this-water-feels-really-really-good* kind of trance.

She'd forgotten she wasn't alone.

"Logan!" she yelled, and glanced behind her at where he stood with his back facing her, both hands over his eyes.

"I'm sorry! I— Why are you taking a bath in your kitchen?!"

"It's also the bathroom," Maddie was still yelling. "Stay turned around!"

"Right!"

"And put the curtain back!"

She watched Logan grope blindly behind him until one of his big hands found the curtain and pulled it closed again. Only then did she let herself relax. Which was the good news. But that also meant she had time to really think about what had just happened.

Which was the bad.

Hurriedly, Maddie stood and rinsed her hair and her body and wrapped herself in a big towel. She was halfway into her base layer when Logan's voice rang out from the other side of the curtain – too close – like he hadn't moved.

"Maddie, why were you taking a bath in the kitchen?"

"Because this is where we heat the water and take the baths. Bath. Room."

"OK," Logan said in the manner of someone who didn't think it was OK at all. "So if this is the bathroom, then where do I—"

Maddie jerked her head through the curtain, then pointed. "It's about forty feet out that door."

Logan looked to the door outside, then back at Maddie. The look that crossed his face in that moment was almost worth having him there, listening to his stupid deep voice and staring at his stupid broad shoulders and putting up with the stupid little jerk that her heart made when he smiled.

"You've got to be kidding me," he muttered.

Maddie smirked. "Welcome to Alaska."

Chapter 7

Dear Logan,

I got all new clothes, which is NOT as exciting as it sounds. Turns out, they don't even make extreme-weather boots with sequins on them. If you ask me, they're missing out on a market. I mean, if you have to be stuck in the mud, shouldn't you at least have something pretty to look at?

Maddie

Going outside at this time of year meant four layers, in Maddie's considerable experience.

Wet layer (waterproof coat, boots).

Dry layer (jeans, flannel shirt).

Base layer (thermal top, leggings).

Under layer (tank top, control-top tights – because in addition to making sure she had a smooth line under her jeans, they were crazy good at preventing friction and holding in body heat, and, in a pinch, Maddie knew she could totally use them to catch fish).

She was just starting to button her shirt when there was a knock on the door. An incredibly loud knock. If it weren't for the fact that their cabin had once held up while there was eight feet of snow on the roof, Maddie might have worried that Logan was getting ready to huff and puff and blow her house down.

But he just knocked again.

"Come in," Maddie said.

"Can I come in?" Logan yelled even though she was 99 percent sure he'd probably heard her.

"I said *come in*!" she shouted. Then, slowly, the doorknob turned.

She recognized the tuft of Logan's dark hair as he leaned inside.

"Well, I didn't want to take any chances."

It wasn't until he actually crossed the threshold that Maddie realized his hand was back over his eyes.

"I'm wearing clothes, Logan," Maddie said, because she absolutely was not going to smile. No. No way. She wasn't going to think that he looked adorable and that he was funny. Funny Logan was shot in a hallway six years ago. Adorable Logan was dead and Maddie would do well to never let herself forget it.

So she just stood there watching as Too-Tall, Too-Big, Too-Grown-Up Logan took his hand off of his eyes and studied her closely, looking from the top of her still-a-little-wet hair to the tips of her really thick socks.

That was when he cocked an eyebrow and asked, "Are you sure you're dressed?"

"What's that supposed to mean?"

One of Maddie's fears – one she had never shared with her father or wrote in her letters or ever, ever voiced aloud – was that she might forget people. How to be with them. How to talk to them. How to read them and make them laugh – that she might forget all the thousands of things that people do and don't say during every day of the world. And that's the fear that hit her right then: that Logan might be talking in a language that she'd forgotten how to speak.

Or maybe it was a language that she had never learned at all.

"I mean . . ." He looked at the green plaid of her flannel shirt. "Don't they make that in pink?"

She finished up the last of the buttons. "No. They don't."

Then Maddie reached for her favorite waterproof jacket, stepped outside, and started pulling on her boots.

"Mad Dog."

"My name is Maddie!" She didn't even realize she was shouting until he stepped back, like she'd slapped him. But Maddie consoled herself with the realization that he absolutely would have known it if she'd slapped him. "Or Madeleine. That's my name. I'd suggest you use it."

"Your dad calls you Mad Dog," Logan told her like it was the most foolproof argument in the world.

She stepped closer. She'd grown a lot in six years, but Logan had grown more. A lot more. She had to crane her neck to look up at him, but still, somehow, she could tell that she made him feel small. "I like my dad."

"So you don't like me?"

"You always were a smart kid, Logan."

With that, she jumped off the porch and stormed down the path towards the water. She saw two tents set up. A pair of Secret Service agents she didn't recognize practically smirked as she passed, like they'd been wanting to yell at Rascal for ages, like they were more than happy to sit aside and let a teenage girl take a stab at him. They looked like they'd even give her the knife.

Which wasn't necessary. Maddie always carried her own.

"I've got chores to do," she told them.

One of them nodded. "We'll be here if you need us."

Maddie turned and started through the woods. A few minutes later she heard heavy feet landing on the cold ground, someone yelling, "Maddie, wait up!"

But Maddie didn't wait up. She was through with waiting: for letters, for phone calls, for people and friends. Maddie was absolutely through with looking back.

"Maddie!" Logan wasn't breathing hard when he caught up with her, but he acted like he was. He'd thrown on his boots and a jacket, but he wasn't ready for Alaska. No one was ready for Alaska on their second day. Ever.

"Where's the fire?" Logan huffed.

"It's back there," Maddie snapped. "And it will go out if we don't get wood."

"There's wood," Logan said.

"There's *never* enough wood." Maddie shook her head like maybe he was the one who didn't understand what words meant.

"Mad Dog— Maddie. I'm sorry. Wait."

But Maddie didn't dare wait. "There's a storm coming, Logan."

"That's the rumor, yes."

"Dad won't be back until after dark – if then. And there's work to do. Lots of work."

"OK, let's work."

She was supposed to make him do it, Maddie knew. And a part of her wanted to make him haul wood and use an ax and climb and claw and dig until his hands bled and his back ached and he would give anything to go back to his big, cushy bed in the most famous house in the world.

But another part of her wanted to turn her back and freeze him out. Freeze him dead.

He slapped his hands together, not to warm them, but to show he was ready for everything. Maddie wanted to laugh. He wasn't ready for anything.

"Just try to keep up."

She turned down a path and started walking. She could feel him on her heels as she shouted back, "Don't wander off by yourself. Especially at night. If you need to go out, tell Dad or take a pistol. Or … on second thought, don't go out at night."

"No nighttime wanderings. Check."

"And don't eat anything you see out here – berries and stuff. Some are delicious. Some will kill you dead."

"Poisonous berries. Check."

Maddie could feel Logan keeping pace just behind her. So she stopped. Spun.

"And whatever you do, don't drink the water. A guide once told Dad that some of the springs still have arsenic in them from the gold rush. I have no idea whether she was joking or not, but let's not risk it, OK?"

"Seriously?" Logan asked. He raised his eyebrows. "Alaska – where even the water will kill you. I'm surprised they don't have that on a T-shirt."

"*Logan*—" Maddie warned. Logan raised his hands in surrender.

"Poisonous water. Check."

She turned and started walking again, trusting him to follow like a shadow.

"And if you see a bear—"

"It's more afraid of me than I am of it," Logan filled in, but Maddie stopped short.

"No." She shook her head and looked at him like he might be a moron, which he probably was. "It's *not* afraid of you. It's a bear! So back away slowly and hope it doesn't want to kill you. Because it can without breaking a sweat."

Logan studied her face, then nodded slowly. "Killer bears. Check."

"And moose," Maddie added. "Moose are the meanest things in Alaska, which is saying something. We don't have a lot of moose around here, but that's just good to know. For the future."

Maddie knew the woods around her. She was aware of every step and rock as they climbed. She knew exactly how the sun would glisten off the lake and how small the cabin would seem when they crested the ridge.

Maddie knew this place, but the boy, she couldn't help thinking, was a stranger.

"Maddie . . ."

"What?" She didn't want to snap, but she really couldn't help herself.

When she looked up at Logan she had to squint against the sun. He was so tall now. So strong. In her memories, he was still a kid with freckles and hair that curled when it got too long. He was still a boy who could see anything and remember everything. But he'd forgotten all about her, and that made all the difference.

"What about you?" he asked. "Are *you* going to kill me?"

Maddie had to think about the answer.

"Why would I do that when I just have to get out of the way and let Alaska do it for me?"

She expected him to turn back after that, thought he might go lumbering down the trail to his Secret Service detail and the satellite phone they no doubt had. She thought he'd go find whatever gadget regular kids were obsessed with that month – or maybe, if he was desperate, a book or a graphic novel or something.

She truly, honestly did not expect him to follow.

She certainly never expected him to say, "You're different."

Maddie stopped and took her hatchet from its sheath, then pulled back her arm and hurled it at a tree thirty feet away. When its blade sank into the bark with a satisfying *thunk* she looked at Logan. "What makes you say that?"

He backed away. "No reason."

There was a dead tree that was small and made good kindling. Maddie hurried to fill her arms with the wood she'd cut a few days before. She couldn't bring herself to face him when she said, "You're different, too."

"I know. I'm way better looking than I used to be."

She could hear the smile in his voice, so cocky but self-deprecating at the same time. It was a special brand of endearing, one you must learn after a lifetime spent in the spotlight, pleasing millions of people. The only person Maddie ever saw was her dad, and she couldn't even please herself most of the time.

So she scanned Logan, from his too-big feet to his still-messy hair. "There was only room for improvement."

Maddie's arms were full and she turned, starting back towards the path and the cabin and whatever she could find to make the day feel a little bit normal.

"My best friend left." Logan's voice sliced towards her on the wind, and something inside of Maddie snapped like the ice on the lake when summer is coming. It felt like she might fall through.

"Don't!" she shouted.

"Don't what?" Logan asked, all innocent.

"Don't act like I left you."

"You *did* leave!" Logan shouted, and Maddie couldn't help herself. She stalked towards him, closer to the edge of the cliff.

"I came here, Logan. This is my life. Look around. These are my friends. This is my school. This is my *life*!" The words echoed across the lake as if they bore repeating, and something in Logan must have known it, sensed it.

Because when he said "Mad ..." his voice broke, but Maddie was the one who felt like crumbling.

And maybe she would have, except a person can't be weak in Alaska. A girl can't cry her way through the long, dark winter because her tears will just freeze on her face and ruin her skin and Maddie had learned that lesson the hard way ages ago.

"Did you even get them?" Maddie asked. "Did you even read them, Logan?"

"Read what?" he asked, and Maddie didn't know whether to scream or push him down the cliff. It would serve him right, she thought. The Secret Service agents probably wouldn't even blame her.

"I wrote you every week. Sometimes more than once

a week. I wrote you every week for *two years*. I wrote you hundreds of letters, and every time my dad would fly home I'd run out to the lake to ask him if you'd written back yet. I'd lie to myself, make believe that I'd probably get all of your letters at once. I was gonna stay up all night reading them. I was going to read them all in order. I was going to make a big list of all the questions you'd ask me and then another list of questions I was going to ask you. I had highlighters. I had stickers. I wrote you every week and then I realized …"

"What?" Logan's voice was small, and Alaska was big. But Maddie heard it anyway.

"It didn't matter that my dad saved your mom that day. It didn't matter that the bullet only grazed you and … It didn't matter. My friend died that day. He died just the same."

"I never got any letters, Maddie."

"Nice try, Logan. You might try that on someone a lot more gullible than I am now."

"No. Seriously. I mean it. I never got any letters!"

"Don't lie to me, Logan. Abandon me. Ignore me – fine. But don't ever lie to me."

"I never got any letters! Maybe my parents—"

"Your mother gave me the stationery! She's the one who told me to write!"

"Maybe the White House thought they were spam or something."

"They weren't emails, Logan. They were *letters*."

"Yeah, but do you have any idea how much mail the White House gets? People write the first family all the time."

"You think I don't know that? You think the former head of your father's security detail didn't double-check the address?"

"I don't know, Mad. Don't hate me. Please. Don't hate me."

Something about the pleading, haunted look in his eyes made Maddie stumble back.

"I don't hate you, Logan. I don't even know you."

And that was so much worse.

"Mad Dog—"

He was reaching for her. He was going to take her hand, maybe smooth her hair. The wind was blowing hard and she hadn't bothered to pull it back. It was still a little damp from her bath, and it was going to be tangled now. It was mistake number eighty-seven for the day, Maddie was starting to realize.

She wasn't going to let number eighty-eight be believing him. Not ever again.

"Maddie, wait!"

Years of rage and pain came boiling up and spilling out. She was a volcano of hurt feelings, and Maddie hated herself for it. But not as much as she hated him.

"You don't get it, Logan. The best thing about my new life was that I never had to see you again."

The first thing you get good at in Alaska is first aid.

There's no nurse's office, no urgent care – no ER just down the road and open twenty-four seven. Maddie could wrap an ankle and treat a burn, and she had never met a splinter she couldn't dig out.

But she'd never seen an injury like what those words did to Logan. And the truth was she had no desire to kiss it and make it better.

"Maddie, look—"

"No, Logan. I don't have to look. I don't have to see. I don't have to ..."

But Maddie's voice trailed off and her anger faded away as she realized that Logan was actually pointing behind her, that he was backing away. Terror filled his face, and it took Maddie a moment to register the look – to remember that it was one she'd seen him wear once before.

Then she heard sounds that had no place in her forest: the snap of a twig beneath a boot; the scrape of a heel over a rock. The skidding of gravel as someone inched too close to the edge.

And Maddie spun just in time to see the butt of a gun slicing towards her. She actually felt the rush of air just before the sharp pain echoed through her face, reverberating down to her spine.

She heard yelling, screaming. And then the sky was too big and blue above her, the ground was rushing up too fast below.

"Maddie, no!" someone yelled, but it must have been a

dream because it sounded just like Logan.

But Logan was gone. Logan was never coming back to her. Ever.

She huddled on the cold ground for a moment, then tried to turn over, maybe get a little more sleep, when she heard the voice in her dream again.

"Maddie, wake up. Maddie, please—"

She tried to rise. She wanted to get up – really, she did. She didn't want to be lazy and spoiled and too weak to survive on her own. But just when she got her hands under her, just when she was starting to push herself from the cold, hard ground a sharp pain slammed into her stomach – it was what Maddie always thought a steel-toed boot might feel like as it connected with a rib.

Yes. That was definitely what it felt like, she thought as she closed her eyes and turned over.

And over.

And over.

And when she finally stopped rolling Maddie didn't fight it anymore. She just let the lights go out.

Chapter 8

Dear Logan,

You know how my dad said he was going to leave the Secret Service because it was dangerous and he didn't want to risk getting killed and leaving me alone in the world and all that?

Well, he brought me to a place where he leaves me alone all the time and where pretty much even the AIR can kill you.

Seriously.

Things that can kill you in Alaska:

– animals

– water

– snow

– ice

– falling trees

– more animals

– bacteria

– the common cold

– *hunger*
– *cliffs*
– *rocks*
– *poorly treated burns, cuts and scrapes*
– *boredom*
I may definitely die of boredom.

Maddie

For a long moment, Logan lay on the cold ground, looking at where Maddie was supposed to be. *She was just there*, he thought, even though the words didn't make any sense. Even though he should have been running, fighting, crawling, or shouting out for help instead of screaming the one word that mattered anymore: "Maddie!"

He was aware faintly of the cold ground beneath his knees, the feeling of rocks biting into his hands as he crawled towards the edge of the cliff.

Maddie was there. He knew it. In the movies, this was when you looked over the side to find a tiny ledge just a few feet down. Maybe she was clinging to a tree – a rock. Something. Anything.

Maddie was down there, and Logan had to get to her. She had to be hanging on.

But there was no ledge. No tree. Logan peered down at the small, twisted body tangled in the brush below. It was probably a fifty-foot fall to the place where she rested. Maybe further.

It was so much further.

But Logan wasn't going to think about that. He could reach her. He could dry all that blood that was over her face. There was so much blood. He could wipe it away and wake her up and they'd laugh about it.

He would tell her he was sorry.

He would. It wasn't too late to say it to her. It wasn't too late. Period.

Logan was so focused on Maddie and her blood and his guilt that he almost forgot about the man.

But when a huge boot landed in the dirt and the rocks in front of him, almost smashing one of Logan's fingers, Logan jerked back.

Slowly, he looked from Maddie's mangled body, up and up until he was squinting against the sun. Only when a head moved to block the light could Logan really see him.

"Shut up," the man said.

But he wasn't a man, really. He probably wasn't even that much older than Logan. In DC, he would have looked like a student at Georgetown, maybe an intern on the Hill. No way the man was older than twenty-five, and if anything he looked younger. He had dark hair a little too long and a dimple in his cheeks.

It was only the eyes. He had old eyes, like they had seen far too much danger and misery to be contained in fewer than twenty-five years.

"Do not move," the man said, and Logan tried to place his accent. Russian, he knew. But which part of Russia? It wasn't the accent of the gutter. No, whoever he was, he'd gone to decent schools. He was important to someone – somewhere. He wasn't some dumb thug with a gun and an ax to grind. No. He sounded like …

He sounded like the men in the corridor – like death itself – and it made Logan shutter and remind himself that this wasn't just another bad dream.

The man's hands were all over Logan then, patting him down and feeling in his pockets. Logan was too stunned to move, but when the man pulled out the small panic button that Logan had sworn to never abandon again, Logan shouted, "No!"

But the man was already pulling back his arm, and Logan watched the button fly over the edge of the cliff.

"Now get up. Slowly." The man climbed off of Logan and backed away, and a part of Logan knew that he was supposed to obey, follow directions. Be good and not make trouble because a grown-up had just given him an order.

But Logan had already forgotten his promise to be good. If anything, he was in the mood to be very, very bad, so as soon as he reached his knees, he put one foot underneath him and shot towards the man's legs, grabbing them in a death grip, twisting and plowing his shoulder into the man's thighs and knocking him to the ground.

Logan wasn't cold anymore. He wasn't hungry or tired or jetlagged. He wasn't even angry. Anger has a beginning and an end. This was simply rage, like a fire had been burning inside of him since he saw his mother's dress sticking out of that rolling cart. This man was nothing but gasoline.

Logan didn't stop until he felt the man hit the ground with a satisfying *thunk*. The two of them rolled, kicking and tangled together. Logan managed to strike the man in the stomach, but it was like he didn't even feel it. The man just reversed their positions and brought the gun up, slamming it into Logan's gut in one fierce blow that made all the breath leave Logan's lungs. Logan turned, wanting to move, to strike. But they'd rolled close to the edge, and when the man pressed, Logan's head turned and there she was.

Maddie.

Not moving.

Face covered with blood.

Maddie was dead, and the realization made Logan's fire go out.

In a flash, the man was up and moving. He held Logan's arm behind his back as he dragged him to his knees, forcing a pair of handcuffs onto one wrist. Too tight.

But Logan couldn't find the words to complain.

All he could say was "You killed her."

The man didn't answer. He just dragged Logan to his feet, pulling his right hand in front of him and cuffing it to his left.

"I should really put your hands behind your back, but if you lose your balance and follow your friend down a ravine it will delay us. We cannot have delays."

"You killed her!" Logan yelled again, lunging forward and smashing his combined wrists against the man's chest, but the blows glanced off like they were nothing. When the gunman looked at Logan he seemed mostly annoyed.

"Yes, I did." The man's voice held no emotion. It was like Logan had asked him for the time, like maybe he was about to comment on the weather. This was just another day in this man's eyes.

Wake up.

Take a walk.

Kill a girl in cold blood.

"You killed her," Logan said again, and suddenly a calm, cold peace came over him. He turned from Maddie's mangled body, and when Logan spoke again, they were the most honest words he'd ever said: "So I'm going to kill you."

The man almost smiled.

"You are welcome to try."

Before Logan could lunge for him again, the man pulled a small silver key from his pocket and dangled it in front of Logan's eyes.

"This is your hope," he said, then brought the key to his lips, kissing it softly. "Good-bye," he said before tossing the key over the edge and into the deep ravine, just like Maddie.

"Maddie."

"Now walk," the man said. He poked Logan in the ribs

with his gun and pushed him in the opposite direction from the cabin.

"You're not going to get it," Logan said. "Whatever you want, if you think kidnapping me is going to help you get it, you're wrong."

"Right now I want you to walk, and I'm going to get that," the Russian said with a shove in Logan's back, forcing his legs under him as gravity took over, pushing him further and further away from Maddie's body.

Maddie's head hurt. And her face felt funny. Like maybe she'd forgotten to take off one of her deep-conditioning masks. Or like maybe the batteries were low and she'd been burning a candle and wax had melted in her hair while she slept. It didn't burn, though. And her skin didn't hurt. But the sticky feeling made her feel like she'd never be clean again, like there wasn't enough water in Alaska to wash it all away.

It was stiff and itchy and ...

She brought her hand to her face, then looked down at her fingers.

Red.

Maddie's hand started to shake. She was too cold, and when she looked at the blood that covered her fingers, she wanted to scream.

Logan.

Maddie remembered fighting with Logan.

She turned and looked up to where she had been – to where he was supposed to be. But the sun was too bright and she had to squint. Her head pounded and all she wanted to do was to lie back down, pillow her aching head on her arm, and go to sleep for an hour. A day. A lifetime.

Nothing would ever feel as good as sleep.

But there was something nagging at her, some thought that wouldn't let her rest.

As soon as she closed her eyes, she saw the gun coming too fast towards her; she felt the blow to her head, the ache of a kick to the gut. And she knew.

"Logan!" she tried, but she couldn't get enough air. All the sound had been kicked right out of her. "Logan!" she tried again, expecting him to peek over the side and tell her it was all some misunderstanding. One of his detail had gotten confused. Someone was going for help. He was going to climb down and get her, grab her in his suddenly-too-strong arms and carry her up the cliff.

She yelled one more time. "Logan!"

And when he didn't answer, she got a whole different kind of worried.

Her head still pounded and her side still ached, but those pains were fading as a new kind of terror took their place.

After all, it was one thing to fall and hit your head in the middle of nowhere. It was another to be knocked unconscious while standing beside the only child of the most powerful man in the world.

"Logan!" she shouted again.

Now wasn't the time to panic.

Now was the time to be smart. Be clever. If Logan was up there, he would have answered by now. Unless he couldn't answer. Unless he was hurt or dead.

But when she saw the red blood on her fingers she couldn't help but think about another piece of red – and instinctively she knew he was alive. After all, plenty of people might want to kill the president. But the president's family? No.

Logan wasn't just a teenager. Logan was *leverage*. And leverage is only worth something when it's alive.

The thought should have been a comfort, but it wasn't. Maybe it was the pounding inside of Maddie's head. More likely, it was the flash she saw on the far side of the river, inching up another ridge, away from the lake and the cabin.

He was there: Logan was *there* and he was alive. But she couldn't tell if there was one gunman with him or two. Or twenty? Maddie cursed herself, utterly unsure. She felt sloppy and stupid and weak, so utterly weak that she could have lain there and wallowed in self-pity for the rest of her life, but she didn't have time for that.

She tried to climb to her feet, but her head swam and she might have been sick if there had been anything in her stomach besides a little coffee and last night's supper.

There was nothing inside of her but fear and regret.

On the far side of the river, Logan stumbled, and the big man hit him in the back, forcing him to climb higher. Faster.

Maddie put her hands to the ground, ready to push herself to her feet, but something cold and sharp bit into her palm. She jerked back, and there, imprinted on the soft flesh of her hand, was a key – a small metal key like to a set of handcuffs. She wanted to scream again because this key on the ground, more than the blood and the pain and the sight of Logan walking away, made it all seem real.

Maddie knew what she had to do. The Secret Service had sent two agents with Logan. Soon they'd be wondering why Rascal hadn't returned. They'd need to check in, touch base. They would be coming. Soon.

And they no doubt had satellite phones and maybe coms units. There was also her dad's old radio and the sat phone he left for emergencies. One way or another, help was waiting at the cabin. She just had to get there and then …

She felt a raindrop.

This happened in Alaska. Clouds could come from nowhere, filling the sky and turning a beautiful day into a deluge in a matter of minutes.

She felt another raindrop. And another. And another.

The soft earth where she'd landed was already starting to form puddles. Whatever trail Logan might be leaving would soon be washed away.

And right then, Maddie knew she had two options.

She could go for help, summon the cavalry and call the guards.

Or there was option two.

How many times had she questioned her father's sanity, wondering what kind of person ran *towards* gunshots?

But the rain was falling harder. So Maddie pulled up the hood of her jacket and watched Logan disappear into the trees and the brush on the opposite rise, and she thought about her father, running towards the gunmen, jumping in front of the bullets.

And Maddie did the only thing she could do: She followed.

Chapter 9

Dear Logan,

When at last we meet again, you should probably know that I'm not the same girl I was when I got here; that's for sure. I've learned a lot. For example:

Things I've learned in Alaska:

1. It's cold.

2. It's wet.

3. Everything is slow.

4. Especially the mail.

Maddie

The summer between eighth grade and Logan's freshman year of high school, he grew four inches and gained thirty-five pounds. Probably another twenty pounds turned from baby fat to muscle, and his feet grew so much his mother started buying his shoes two sizes too big. The president used to joke that it was going to impact the national debt just to feed him.

It wasn't fun. And it wasn't funny. Not for Logan, at least. It was like going to bed one night and waking up every morning in an entirely different body – one that didn't move the same, feel the same, work in the same way as the one he had always known. His fingers were clumsy and his feet were clunky and it felt like he was constantly at risk of moving too fast in the wrong direction and toppling over. It seemed to take months for his center of gravity to feel like his own again.

This is what that felt like.

Walking through the woods, still numb and angry, his hands bound in front of him as he plodded up a hill and over the rough ground, Logan's feet were heavier than they should have been. He stumbled and shuffled and dragged his new all-terrain boots over terrain that he never before could have dreamed of.

Logan was in good shape. He played sports in school and liked to swim and play basketball games with the off-duty Secret Service agents who always seemed to be hanging around the court at the White House.

But he was tired. He was winded. He wanted to sit down and stare forever.

He wanted Maddie back.

He'd just gotten Maddie back.

Logan didn't care when he ran into a tree limb and broke it, when he kicked a rock and sent it down the steep face of the hill, lost in the mud and muck.

It was starting to drizzle, but he barely felt it. Logan

barely felt anything. At least he didn't until the man with the gun started to laugh.

"What's so funny?" Logan spat out the words, rainwater clinging to his mouth and spewing forth like he might be rabid.

But the kidnapper smiled. "You. Thinking you are going to leave a trail for someone to follow. You have seen too many movies, my friend."

"I'm not your friend."

"No. You are my hostage. Walk."

Logan turned and did as he was told, but he couldn't shut up. That was asking too much. His hands were starting to go numb, and he had to use his arms and lean at the waist to try to get enough momentum to drag his body upward.

"Do you really think no one is going to miss me? I thought you knew who I was. People tend to notice if the first kid goes AWOL."

"There is no one to miss you."

Now Logan wanted to laugh. "I'm the president's only child. When Maddie and I don't come back, they'll have an army in these woods. They'll have *the* Army."

He spun on the man, feeling triumphant, but the feeling turned to ice as a cold, cruel grin spread across the man's face.

"Are you thinking of the men in your camp or of your little friend?" the man asked, then shook his head. "It does not matter. Like I said, there is *no one* to miss you."

Suddenly, the ground moved, the earth shifted. Logan blamed it on the wet, steep hillside, but it was more than that.

Charlie had gotten fired because of him, but in that moment, Logan knew that the two agents who'd been forced to follow him to Alaska had gotten much, much worse.

He could barely get the question out: "What did you do?"

"What I've only begun to do. Now walk." The Russian accent seemed thicker now, with this new, awful knowledge. "We cannot fall behind schedule."

He reached for Logan then, to grab him by the handcuffs and jerk him to his feet, toss him around as if he weighed nothing – was nothing.

But even as the clouds grew thicker, Logan's mind grew clearer. He could see it now: what had happened – what *was* happening. The Russian was right about one thing: Logan had watched a lot of movies, and he knew that there would be no negotiating for his freedom, no tearful, tense exchange. He'd seen this man's face; he'd heard his voice. Logan was a dead man. Just like the two agents who had brought him here.

Just like Maddie.

Maddie.

Logan heard a fierce roar that rumbled like thunder in the dense woods, but it wasn't a bear – it was his own mangled cry. He didn't think or feel or worry anymore.

He just lunged at the man who was standing beneath him on the hillside.

Maddie was dead. And something inside of Logan was alive and fighting, and he didn't want it to stop until these woods were covered with blood.

He felt the man falling and grabbed hold tighter, and the two of them rolled over and over across the rocks. Tree limbs slashed against them. Logan tasted blood. His screams filled the air, a terrible piercing cry that he didn't even try to stop.

His hands were still cuffed, and he slammed them into the man's gut, pounding like a hammer with both fists. The man was dazed, but he wasn't stopped, and when Logan pulled back again, the Russian moved like a blur, reversing their positions and leaping to crouch over Logan, pressing his chest against the rocky ground.

Logan never even saw the knife.

Not until he felt it, cutting into the soft flesh between his pinkie finger and its neighbor. At first, his hands were too cold, too numb, and Logan was too high on adrenaline and anger to feel any pain. But then he saw the bright red drop of blood that bubbled up from his too-white skin.

He felt the kidnapper's warm breath on his cold cheek, heard the accented warning: "This is not the part of you I need," the man whispered near Logan's ear. "Now you must ask yourself: Do you want to lose more than just your girlfriend and your pride today?"

The man seemed to think he'd asked an excellent

question, made an undeniable point. He didn't know that Logan had already lost everything that meant anything to him. A pinkie finger was the least of his problems.

No. The only thing Logan cared about was vengeance. And he wasn't going to get that – not right then; not right there. He wasn't going to get Maddie back with his bare fists. He had to …

I am never going to get Maddie back, Logan realized.

It was suddenly harder than it should have been to keep breathing.

The man dragged him to his feet, pushed him in the back.

"Now walk."

Maddie knew her way across the river. Even cold and hungry and still a little too unsteady on her feet, she'd crossed the old fallen tree enough times to know that it could hold her.

The man hadn't known about it, though. Or maybe he hadn't wanted to risk climbing down the steep cliff face to reach it. In any case, by Maddie's estimation she'd gained at least an hour on them. But she'd probably been unconscious at least that long, so she didn't know how much good it did her. Besides, her head hurt too badly to think too much. So she just kept walking.

When she reached the place where riverbank gave way

to trees, Maddie saw the broken branches. Even with the rain, someone had dug so deeply into the soft earth while searching for footing that it was almost impossible to miss the ruts. Now.

Maddie looked up at the sky, at the clouds that were growing thicker, darker. Maybe it was the drizzle that clung to her hair or the shock from her long, hard fall, but it was definitely getting colder. And it was going to get a whole lot worse before it got better. In a lot of ways.

Someone might miss Logan's tracks if they didn't know where to look for them – if the weather kept getting worse. So Maddie walked to the river and gathered the biggest rocks she could, then placed them like an arrow, pointing the way. She piled a few smaller stones on top, just high enough to be noticed in a few inches of snow and ice, but not so high that they might topple.

Then Maddie lowered her hood. She brought her hand to the side of her face and pressed her palm against the largest of the rocks until her bloody handprint shone like an eerie beacon, announcing to the world: *Trouble came this way*.

But trouble was Maddie's family's business, so she did the only thing that made sense: She followed it.

The footprints were easy to track for a while, but then the ground got rockier and the rain got harder. Luckily there were a lot of trampled bushes and broken branches. It looked like a bulldozer had passed that way, and a part of her wondered if Logan was doing it on purpose. She didn't know him well enough to say anymore, and that hurt almost as much as her head.

She could feel the swelling beneath her hair, but that was good, wasn't it? Better for it to swell out than in? Maybe her brain would be OK even if her hair would look terrible. Maddie consoled herself with the fact that there wouldn't be anyone around to see it. That and the whole life-and-death thing.

That's what made her bend at the waist and leverage herself higher. And higher. The rain was still falling, but she was making good time.

Her shoulder hurt, though, probably from the fall. And sometimes she'd find herself stopping, wincing, because it felt like a sword was going between her ribs, but she was pretty sure they weren't broken – just bruised.

It could be worse, she told herself.

She could have left home without a raincoat like a moron.

Was Logan wearing a raincoat? Maddie couldn't remember. She just knew he was a moron, and the thought should have worried her, but she just smiled a little. Logan was gone without a trace and she was calling him a moron in her mind.

Things were almost back to normal.

But then Maddie saw something on the hill – an overturned rock, like someone had struggled to make a step.

Not quite a moron, she told herself, and went to the

rock, stacked a half dozen others around and on top of it with a small limb sticking straight up for good measure, and then she started up the hill again, certain that she was on the right path.

She wanted to run. She wanted to find him and make sure he was OK and just have the worrying part behind her.

But she also had to be careful, be quiet. If the man thought she was dead, then that could be her best weapon. She'd left her second-favorite hatchet stuck blade-deep in a tree at the top of the cliff, after all. So she stayed quiet, even though that came with its own set of problems.

As Maddie pushed through a piece of heavy brush, she heard a sound that sometimes haunted her nightmares.

Part grunt. Part growl.

Maddie froze on the path as the bear pivoted and saw her. It must have smelled her or heard her messing with the rocks and cursing Logan under her breath. Because, thankfully, it wasn't scared. It had known she was there, even if Maddie couldn't say the same.

It was covered in thick fur, fat and ready for winter as it rubbed up against a tree like it had an itch it couldn't quite scratch. But it didn't charge at her. If anything, it seemed annoyed that she'd intruded on its solitude. So Maddie did the only thing she could do – she put her hand on the hilt of her knife, then eased back, slowly slipping away.

When her heart returned to its chest, she veered off the beaten path but kept climbing.

She didn't stop to think about the truth of her situation: There were two predators in these woods, and Maddie wasn't sure which one scared her most.

Chapter 10

Dear Logan,

Alaska's really big.

And really pretty.

It's also really lonely.

Sometimes I ask Dad why we're here and he says it's for our health. Or because I'm almost old enough that he was going to have to "beat the boys off with sticks" if we'd stayed in DC. I don't think that's it, though. But if it is, he's found the place where the stick-to-boy ratio is probably the highest on earth.

Maddie

Logan didn't know what time it was. Usually he was good about stuff like that: finding north, knowing how much daylight must be left. Maybe it was from spending so much of his life surrounded by the Secret Service. Logan had received more than a few lessons from well-meaning agents on knowing when someone looks out of place in a crowd or when a vehicle just doesn't quite fit in.

Someone had even told him once that if his father hadn't been president, Logan might have been a good candidate for the Blackthorne Institute (whatever that was – it didn't even have a website), so it felt weird not knowing where he was or where he was going.

When Logan remembered how far north they were and how close they were to the shortest day of the year, he had to wonder how much daylight even remained. He knew there were parts of Alaska that didn't get any sun at all in the middle of winter and some that got a few hours. Some got more. But Logan didn't know that much about this part of the state. Alaska was more than twice the size of Texas, after all. And then Logan had to hand it to the man at his back: There was no better place to get lost.

Maybe that was why it took him a moment to realize that someone was talking.

It took a moment more to realize that no one was talking to him.

Logan turned slowly. The storm had broken for a moment, and a rare bit of sunlight broke through the heavy canopy of the trees.

Some rainwater puddled on the ground, and Logan realized that it had started to freeze. Now that they weren't moving he could feel it: The air wasn't just chilly anymore; it was downright cold. He stomped his feet and wanted to put his hands in his pockets, but they were still cuffed in front of him and growing numb. Logan had no idea if it was from the tight cuffs or the cold air. It didn't matter. It was the same person's fault either way.

"*Nyet*," the man said, and something about it made Logan want to laugh.

Then Logan saw the telephone.

And he actually wanted to laugh harder.

"There's no signal, dude!" he yelled. The words seemed to echo in the vast wilderness.

"Shut up!" the man spat in English, then turned his back to Logan.

He put the satellite phone to his ear and started talking fast and in Russian, and something in the sound of those guttural vowels and consonants made Logan shiver in a way that had nothing to do with the cold.

He remembered the feel of his shoulder hitting the wall as the men rushed down the center of the corridor. The flutter of a red dress. The piercing pain of the bullet slicing across his arm. The blood.

And the sounds of Maddie's screams.

Maddie.

Maddie was gone. She'd been gone for what felt like ages, it was true. But now she was the kind of gone he couldn't pretend away. He'd just gotten her back, and this man had taken her from him.

"I just got her back!"

Logan didn't even realize he was yelling until the man spun and stared at him. The phone was to his ear, and now that he was facing Logan, Logan could hear every word.

Logan's Russian wasn't perfect, but he recognized "*Yes, I have the boy*" when he heard it.

Logan wanted to smile at the words – not at what they were, but that he'd understood them.

The morning after That Night, Logan's dad had pushed Logan's wheelchair down the hall to see Maddie's dad. Afterward, on the ride back, Logan had turned to his father and said, "I'm going to learn Russian."

His dad was still running a hand over the resignation letter that Mr Manchester had given him, handwritten on hospital stationery. He must have understood what was happening – how much everything was going to change, even if Logan didn't yet realize that the president losing the head of his Secret Service detail meant the first son was also going to lose his best friend.

"Did you hear me?" Logan had said. "I'm going to learn Russian."

"OK," his father had told him. "Go ahead."

So he had. It was perhaps the one good decision Logan had ever made in his life. At least it was the only one that seemed worthwhile in that moment.

"*Yes. I am certain we will not be followed*," the kidnapper said. He looked directly into Logan's eyes, and Logan tried to keep the same look of enraged indifference that he'd had before. He couldn't let on that he understood. It might be the only weapon he had, and he wasn't going to lose it too soon.

"*Is the plane ready?*" the kidnapper asked. "*We will be*

there. You just make sure we have a doctor."

Only the last part surprised Logan, and he made a conscious effort to school his features, hide his reaction. Once he thought about it, it made a kind of sense. Logan wasn't really hurt yet, after all. But if he kept annoying this guy, he would be. And whoever this man was working for – whatever their motivation might be – no one drags the president's son through the wilderness in a storm if they don't need him alive.

They need me alive, Logan thought, but it didn't bring him any comfort. They thought he might be a pawn, a useful tool. They thought he had value. Logan would have laughed if it hadn't been so funny.

Instead, he just said, "He hates me."

The man took off his pack, slipped the satellite phone into a side pocket, and quickly drew the zipper shut – but not before Logan noted which pocket the phone was in.

It was like he hadn't spoken at all – like maybe he was the one speaking in another language, so he said again, louder, "He hates me!"

Finally the man looked up, and Logan couldn't help but cock an eyebrow, careful not to tip his hand.

"That was a ransom call, wasn't it?" Logan lied, and Maddie's killer seemed pleased to realize that the first son was as stupid as everyone said. It had always been in Logan's best interest to keep it that way. Now more than ever.

"If that was a ransom call, I hope you asked for a miracle,

because the president of the United States *hates* me."

Maybe it sounded like fear, or anger, or moody teenage angst, but Logan wasn't really ready for the sight of the Russian dropping to a log and asking, "So are you saying I should just kill you now?"

"No." Logan shook his head. "I'm saying you should let me go. You see, he doesn't actually care what happens to me. But he would care a great deal if he were to be *embarrassed*. If someone took something that belongs to him, he'd need to make an example out of that somebody. So you'd be better off just letting me go."

The kidnapper studied Logan, as if maybe the intelligence he'd been given was off – like maybe the first son wasn't just sloppy and stupid, like maybe he might also be a little bit insane.

That was OK, Logan thought. There were times when insanity could be very beneficial.

"If you're right and there's no one looking for me, then that means no one knows I'm missing. *Yet*. If you let me go, it might stay that way for a while. You could be long gone, back to wherever you came from, before anyone even starts to care."

The man leaned closer, his accent heavier. "*I* will care."

Logan shook his head, like this man with the knife and the gun – this man who had hit Maddie in the head and kicked her in the gut, then pushed her off the edge of a cliff like she was a pebble and he wanted to see how far she would fly … Logan looked at him like *he* was the weak one, the one destined for disappointment.

When the words came, they were actually filled with pity. "You're not going to get what you want."

But the Russian stood slowly and leaned closer. "I already have what I want."

For a second, Logan actually believed him. It took a moment for him to remember.

"You don't seem to understand how this hostage business works. See … you take me. Then you trade me for something infinitely more valuable."

"Get up," the man said, as if Logan hadn't spoken at all. "We have lost too much light already."

That was when Logan realized that the sun wasn't where it should be. The days were so short; Logan had no idea what time it was. He only knew that when he started to stand, his head pounded. The earth tilted. And the meal he'd shared with Maddie and her father last night seemed forever ago.

"Move!" the man shouted.

Logan didn't want to do anything, but he knew he couldn't just sit there – he couldn't just die there. Because then he wouldn't be able to kill this man later.

So he swallowed his pride and asked, "Do you have anything to eat?"

"We eat when we rest. We rest when we lose the light."

"That's a great plan," Logan told him. "But I didn't

have breakfast and we're not going to make any time until I get a little gas in the tank. I'm no good to you this way."

The thing that Logan hated the most was how much that was true. Maybe that's why the man believed him, because a moment later he was swinging off his pack and digging through a compartment, then tossing Logan something that looked like an energy bar. The writing was in Russian, some brand name Logan didn't know. But he ripped open the package and dug in, eating just the same.

"You eat while we walk," the man said, pushing Logan up the hill.

"What? No beverage? I was hoping for a nice latte."

The Russian threw him a canteen so quickly that Logan was actually surprised he caught it.

"Now walk," the man said.

Maddie was surprised when she finally heard the talking.

It had been so long since she'd been used to any kind of voices. That was the weirdest thing about her new life: It wasn't just the lack of people – it was the lack of sound. There was no radio in her world. No television. No YouTube or whatever Internet thing kids were into. A dozen different fads could have come and gone and Maddie wouldn't have even known they existed.

Sure, her dad brought her newspapers and magazines.

Sometimes she watched movies that they had on DVD. She had her mom's old CD collection, and sometimes when Maddie was all alone she'd blast the soundtracks from nineties movies just as loud as she could and dance around the cabin like no one was watching. Because no one was.

But most days, Maddie's world was silent except for the sound of birds and running water, chainsaws and the crack a tree makes just before it falls.

Voices didn't belong in that forest, but when Maddie heard them, they sounded like music.

Because the voices meant Logan was still alive.

Of course, if he kept talking to the man that way he wouldn't be for long. Maddie took some degree of comfort from the knowledge that she probably wasn't the only person in those woods who really, really wanted to kill him.

When Logan shouted, "I just got her back!" something inside of Maddie froze. She wondered for a moment if maybe she'd spent too long away from civilization. Maybe some words changed meaning while she was away because Logan sounded like someone who had just lost his very best friend.

Maddie might have felt sorry for him if she hadn't lost her own best friend years ago.

She made herself stay in the shelter of the trees, listening. Watching.

Logan is alive, Maddie thought again, and for the first

time in hours she really let herself breathe.

He seemed more mad than afraid. She'd never seen him look like that before. But maybe he looked like that all the time now. Maybe this was how he did teenage angst. Maybe all boys did. It's not like she knew anyone to compare him to.

But no. It was more than that. Logan was going to kill the man who'd taken him.

Kill the man who'd hurt *her*.

And right then Maddie's biggest worry was making sure he didn't get himself killed first.

Logan ran his sleeve over his mouth. Or sleeves, rather. His hands were still cuffed, and he kept the energy bar in one, the canteen in the other. He had a feeling he should be savoring this, committing the feel of food and water to memory. He might not taste either one again for a very long time.

"So what's your name?" Logan wanted to sound casual, maybe crazy. A sane person would be terrified by now, he knew, ranting and rambling and promising to give the man with the gun anything he wanted.

But Logan had learned a long time ago that there was nothing you could give a man with a gun to make him happy. Men with guns were only satisfied when they *took*. And Logan was going to hang on to the last of his self-respect for as long as he possibly could.

So he took another bite and asked, "Is it Jimmy?" Logan plastered on a smile and looked back over his shoulder at the man who might have been his shadow if the sun hadn't gone back behind the clouds.

"Bob?" Logan guessed again. "Matthew, Mark, Luke? John? Larry? Steve?" He watched the man closely, and when the Russian's eye twitched Logan was so proud of himself for seeing it that he might have laughed. "It's Stefan, isn't it?"

Stefan didn't answer, but he didn't have to. Logan already knew he was right.

He took a big bite of his bar and turned to keep on walking. "I met some of your countrymen once. Well, I didn't so much meet them as I watched them try to kidnap my mother."

"Keep walking." The words were meant to be a jab in the back, but Logan didn't much care. Somewhere in that big wilderness there was a plane waiting on them. And a doctor just in case. Whatever his final destination, it probably wouldn't be as cozy as the middle of those trees and rocks, lost among the rain and the temperatures that were both falling too fast for comfort. Somehow, Logan knew that very shortly this place and time might feel like a vacation.

"These bars are good. You want a bite?"

"Shut up!" Now Stefan was the one who looked like he was stuck somewhere he didn't want to be, doing something he didn't want to do.

Logan shook his head. "Manners, Stefan."

But it was a mistake, because in an instant the knife was out. "Do you think you are cute? Funny? I need you, but I do not need your tongue. In fact, I see a great deal of benefit in relieving you of it right here. Right now."

A kind of wet-weather creek had sprung up during the storm as rainwater collected on the hillside, racing down towards the river below. When Stefan stepped forward, his foot landed in the water, but it was like he didn't even feel the chill. His rage was so hot that Logan half expected to see steam.

Logan held his hands up, stepped away. "Hey, I'm just making an honest offer."

Stefan glared. "I'm making an honest threat."

"I can see that," Logan said somberly. "You're obviously a man of your word."

"Walk," Stefan ordered, and Logan did as he was told.

It was only after a few steps that he exhaled, suddenly grateful that there wasn't a knife in his back.

"So just out of curiosity, what do you think I'm worth?" he asked when he just couldn't help himself. "I mean, it isn't often a person's put on the open market. What is the going rate for presidents' sons these days? Is it more or less than what you guys were going to get for my mother? Accounting for inflation, of course."

Logan didn't know what to expect: The knife? The gun? Maybe a nice hard shove into freezing water? He couldn't have been more surprised when the man said, "I did not take your mother."

"I know you didn't," Logan told him. "You were what? My age then?"

He wasn't much more than a kid now, Logan tried to remind himself. But kids are sent into war zones every day. Kids can be psychopaths. Kids can kill.

Stefan straightened. "If I had tried to take your mother, she would have been taken."

It wasn't a boast. It wasn't a threat. It was a simple fact of life, and Logan couldn't keep from saying, "I believe you."

"Good. Now walk."

The man stepped in front of Logan, as if to lead the way.

But with every step the echoing pulse that had been beating inside Logan's head for hours grew louder and louder.

Maddie is dead.

Maddie is dead.

Maddie is—

When Logan stumbled over one of the big rocks near the stream, his hands plunged into the freezing water, breaking his fall.

Maddie is dead, he thought one more time.

Before Logan even realized what he was doing, his cuffed hands were digging into the ground. He was kicking at the rock that was big, but not too big. It was jagged, and even with his cold hands Logan could feel the sharp, perfect edges.

With the sound of the rain hitting the leaves and the gurgling stream it was almost too easy to sneak up on the man. Logan knew he had one shot. If Stefan didn't go down immediately, there'd be a fight, and then the knife and the gun would come into play. Which was fine. Logan didn't care about getting stabbed, getting shot. Logan only cared about the weight of the stone and the timing of his step.

He raised his arms high overhead, said a prayer—

And saw it.

He had to blink, certain that it was a mirage – a sign. But it wasn't the kind of sign he was expecting, so he stepped a little closer, certain that there couldn't really be a piece of gold dangling from a tree limb, there in the middle of a storm in the middle of nowhere.

Had Stefan seen it? Maybe he thought it strange but insignificant.

After all, he hadn't chosen that charm bracelet six years ago, placed it on his best friend's wrist.

He didn't know to stand in the rain and whisper, "Maddie."

Logan told himself that she must have left it there, lost it ages ago.

But no. The bracelet was too clean and the forest was too large and the girl was too tough to die that easily. Logan should have known.

"What are you doing back there?" Stefan's voice came cutting through the mist, so Logan dropped the rock and grabbed the bracelet.

He held the canteen to the leaves that were dripping rainwater like a fountain.

"Refilling the canteen!" he shouted.

"Less water. More walking," the big Russian yelled.

Stefan didn't see the way Logan scanned the woods around them, looking for a girl who was far too careful to be seen.

He had no idea he was outnumbered.

Chapter 11

Dear Logan,

I'm very sorry to hear that you are in a coma.

Or maybe you have amnesia.

Or you lost the use of your writing hand and are learning to write with your other hand, which we both know would be saying something since even with your good hand your penmanship is atrocious.

Or, wait, maybe the White House is out of paper.

Oh my gosh! Is the White House out of paper?! You'd think that would be in the newspapers that my dad brings, but I could see where it might be a national security risk. No wonder the press is keeping it hush-hush.

Don't worry. Your secret is safe with me.

Who am I going to tell?

Maddie

Logan's coat was red. Which was a good thing. For now. There's a reason the redcoats were pretty much doomed during the American Revolution. He stood out like a beacon among the huge trees and big rocks and leaf-covered ground that was getting slicker and slicker with every passing moment.

So Maddie didn't have to get too close to keep them in her sights. Plus, Logan must have made it his mission to kick every rock and break every branch he came across. Maddie was glad of it. As soon as the agents realized he was missing they should be able to track him down.

If the agents realized soon.

If the light held.

If the tracks didn't wash away.

If the whole forest didn't fall asleep beneath a blanket of snow and ice.

Someone has to come help, she wanted to scream.

Someone other than Maddie.

She heard the man yell something at Logan – "Less water. More walking."

And the air around Maddie got even colder. She knew the accent even if she didn't know the voice. It was one she still heard sometimes in her nightmares. On those nights, Maddie slept with her back to the wall and her hatchet by her bed. If her ghosts followed Maddie to Alaska, that was fine, she told herself. She was going to be ready.

But now she was hunching down behind a fallen log

and watching as Logan and the kidnapper kept going.

But Logan had stopped. And turned. And Maddie knew he'd found the bracelet.

Which meant Phase One was working. If Logan knew she was alive and she was here, then maybe he would stop acting like an idiot who didn't care if he got himself killed.

It had taken all of Maddie's strength not to scream when Logan had picked up the rock and crept towards the gunman's back. Logan was ready to kill, and Maddie couldn't blame him. In Alaska, people hunted to survive all the time. But Alaska was also the kind of place where being stupid would kill *you*, and Maddie knew they might have only one chance. They had to make the most of it.

When Logan's red coat moved farther out of sight, Maddie left her hiding place and went to the deep tracks that Logan had left in the muddy ground. Then she picked up the end of the log she'd been hiding behind. It had been down for years, she could tell, rotting and decaying in the near constant moisture, and it was almost light as Maddie picked it up and swung it around. She dragged her knife through the bark, drawing an arrow and pointing the way.

Her dad would know that the log had been disturbed. Even if snow gathered on the top, any idiot would be able to see the arrow on the side, high enough that the snow and ice shouldn't cover it.

Someone had to see it.

Maddie told herself that her father would be landing

soon. Logan's detail was probably out right then, searching and calling for reinforcements.

Soon. Someone would catch up with her soon.

Unless her dad's job had complications …

Unless his plane broke down or the storm came in faster than anyone was expecting …

Unless no one realized they should be looking in *this* direction …

Unless somehow, for some reason, she couldn't keep Logan in her sights …

Help has to come, Maddie told herself for what had to be the thousandth time.

But there are things you tell yourself. And there are things you *know*. And Maddie knew that the only person she could depend on was herself.

But that's OK, she thought. *I'm usually enough*.

Maddie took one last look at the marker she was leaving behind, then pulled her hood tighter around her face and started up the hill.

She had to keep up. Or, better, get ahead. The best hunting always happened when the prey came to you. Maddie could lie in wait. She could be prepared. She could have a plan and then hope and pray that Logan's stupid boy brain and stupid boy ego didn't get in the way of what she already knew would be a perfectly logical, smart-girl plan.

But first Maddie had to figure out *where*.

Not where Logan and the kidnapper were. But where

Logan and the kidnapper were *going to be*.

That was Phase Two. And without Phase Two there could never, ever be a Phase Three. Which was important because Phases Four through Twenty were pretty much "hope" and "pray" and "try to get really, really lucky."

"Where are you ...?"

Maddie trailed off when she heard the sound of the water. The hill they were on was steep and rough, and one whole side was more like a cliff than a mountain. As Maddie crept towards it, she knew even before she pushed aside the thick green branches of the evergreens what she was going to see.

This part of Alaska was full of rivers and streams – massive ravines cut by glaciers centuries ago and dug deeper by the water that ran through them almost all year long.

The waterfall was proof of that.

The kidnapper could hide out in this forest for days if he wanted to. The Secret Service would have satellites trained on the cabin, but the mountains were covered with trees. As long as they kept walking – kept covered – then they were invisible from the sky. Which was smart. But the kidnapper had to know that someone would find them eventually. Logan was the president's son, after all. People would be looking. Lots of people. And soon.

So they had to be planning to get Logan out of there. Out of Alaska. Judging by the kidnapper's thick accent, probably even out of the country. After all, Russia was pretty close. Closer than the rest of the US.

But there were no roads in this part of Alaska. Which meant they had to take Logan out by boat or by plane, and they were moving away from the coast, which meant plane.

Which meant …

Maddie looked back at the waterfall, the deep, rough ravine that ran between the mountains, and just like that she knew where they were going – and what she had to do.

But *how* – how was another question entirely.

She was so busy thinking, running through options and possibilities, pros and cons, that she didn't pay attention to where she was stepping, not until it was totally too late.

Maddie heard the snap almost at the same moment that she felt the pain.

And then she found herself leaping, falling, and skidding across the uneven ground and rolling through the mud and the muck. Water was seeping through her jeans, and Maddie knew she needed to get her feet under her but her left leg felt like it was on fire.

It wasn't, though. It was just cut and bleeding. Her jeans were ripped and Maddie was almost afraid to pull back the denim and examine the deep stab wound in the side of her calf. But it wasn't as bad as it could have been. Maddie knew this like she knew her own name.

In a weird way, she'd been lucky, Maddie realized as she forced herself upright and hobbled to the old, rusty trap that had been set at some point in the past fifty years and then abandoned. The mechanism must have rusted through the decades. That's why Maddie had a flesh wound and not a leg that would never really work right again.

For a second, she just stood there, breathing too hard, feeling lucky to be alive.

Then her breath grew deeper and her heart started beating hard for an entirely different reason.

She might be bloody and hungry and covered with mud. She might not have friends, teachers, classes, cell coverage, adequate food (for the moment), or any prayer of finding help anytime soon.

But – Maddie smiled – she *did* have a plan.

Chapter 12

Dear Logan,

It's been two years. Seven hundred and thirty days since I sent my first letter. I'm not going to lie to myself anymore. You probably think you're too important to bother writing me back. I guess you lied, too, when you said we'd be friends forever.

I've learned a lot since I moved to Alaska, but the most important thing is this: Any friend who doesn't write back isn't your friend at all.

So goodbye from Alaska, where I am the most important person for twenty miles in any direction.

(I'm the only person for twenty miles in any direction.)

Maddie

Logan had thought he couldn't get any wetter or any colder, but he'd been wrong. So very, very wrong. Like the kind of wrong he was when he had bet Maddie that he could eat all the ice cream in the White House deep freeze and then found out they were preparing for a state dinner and had a hundred gallons.

He made it through half of one huge tub before she took pity on him and made him stop.

He never wanted to feel that way again, but Logan was so cold, so sick. His feet hurt and his head hurt and that energy bar had turned to acid in his stomach. He might have thought Stefan had poisoned him except he knew for certain that Stefan's bosses were going to need him alive.

When the man pulled to a sudden stop, Logan almost knocked into him.

When Stefan said "We rest here," Logan almost wanted to cry with relief. It was only the weight of Maddie's bracelet in his pocket that kept him going.

He was walking as slowly as he could, but they'd been going for hours. More than once, he'd started to just sit down, stop walking. But Maddie was out there somewhere. Watching. Logan wasn't about to let her see him cry.

As soon as the kidnapper slid off his pack and sank onto a huge boulder, Logan dropped to a fallen tree.

On any other day, Logan might have walked from the clearing and looked out over the huge hills and narrow valleys, the massive wilderness that spread out before him like something from a movie. He was on an epic quest, he told himself. Any moment now, reinforcements were going to show up and he was going to save the maiden in distress.

But Logan had to laugh when he realized that *he* was the maiden in this scenario. And he didn't care one bit.

When the phone started ringing, it was a sound from another century – another world. *There are no phones in Mordor*, Logan wanted to snap before he realized: *It's the phone.*

"*Da*," the kidnapper said, answering it. He didn't bother to turn away from Logan, lower his voice.

"*Get here!*" the man shouted. Even if he hadn't understood every word, Logan would have known that Stefan was angry. Something wasn't going according to plan.

"*No!*" Stefan snapped. "*A boat will take too long. We cannot reach the coast now. There is no time. We must have the plane and the doctor.*"

A beat passed while Stefan listened and Logan worried.

Whatever the person on the other end of the line was saying, it made Stefan stare at Logan, not just with hatred, but with fury. As if Logan had personally killed his dog, burned his house, and ruined his future. Logan was the thing that went bump in the night as far as Stefan was concerned, and Logan made a point of remembering that – of reminding himself that maybe not everyone wanted him taken alive.

"*No. Everything is perfect on this end*," Stefan said into the phone in Russian. Logan tried hard not to smile at the sarcasm he wasn't supposed to understand.

But he must have failed because Stefan snapped, "What?"

Logan shook his head. "It's rude to have conversations in front of people without including them. I'm kind of an expert, you see, because when I was seven my parents got me an etiquette tutor. And, you know, if there's one thing seven-year-old boys love, it's etiquette."

Logan smiled his too-bright smile, but Stefan only scowled.

"You should rest your mouth while you're resting your feet."

When the man hung up the phone and put it back in his pack, he pulled the zipper halfway.

But only half.

Logan could have sworn he'd done it on purpose, like eating in front of a starving man.

Then Stefan pulled a map from his pack and spread it on the nearest boulder. The map was laminated and unfolded into probably twenty squares.

"Can I have the canteen?" Logan asked as he stood and walked towards Stefan and his map.

"Here." Stefan shoved the canteen at him and Logan took it. He drained it in one long gulp, then handed it back, lingering a little too long over the map as he did so.

The map's creases gave it something of a grid-like pattern, which was great as far as Logan was concerned. He liked things tidy and straight and neat.

He liked things he could memorize.

He wasn't there more than ten seconds. Fifteen maybe. And Stefan never even got suspicious.

Maybe I'll join the CIA after this, Logan thought. *Or maybe I'll lock myself in my room and never leave again*.

He was turning, he was thinking, when a gust of wind blew through the trees. Rain hit him hard, and the temperature seemed to drop instantly to below freezing. It was like winter decided to wake up and blow out its birthday candles. The rain suddenly burst from the clouds, thicker and colder, and Logan squinted for a moment, as if maybe he could shake his head and open his eyes again and find it had all been a very bad dream.

But it wasn't a dream. It was a nightmare. When the wind blew again, it caught the map and whipped it off the rock and across the clearing.

They were in the middle of millions of acres of wilderness – no roads, no mile markers, and absolutely no cell signal. Google Maps would never get them to the airplane Stefan was so desperate to meet.

He needed that map.

So Stefan ran, chasing it like it was a butterfly flitting and floating on the freezing wind.

Logan didn't think about it. It wasn't a strategy or a plan. He only knew that Stefan was busy and his pack was sitting, abandoned, by the boulder.

The pack that had the satellite phone in it.

Logan didn't think at all, he just moved. Instinct taking over, the fight for survival warring with the fight for being smart.

But maybe *this* was smart. Maybe this was the right move at the right time. He didn't know. Didn't really care.

He just knew that he had to *do something*, and he was reaching into the half-zipped pocket of the pack – pulling the satellite phone free – before he could even blink. He almost had it in his own pocket when he felt something ram into his side like he'd just been hit by a bus.

He fell hard, but the ground was soft enough that the only thing that really hurt was his pride.

That was before Stefan managed to roll them again. Logan elbowed him in the ribs, but a moment later he was pinned against the ground, Stefan's heavy weight on top of him. Logan lashed out. He remembered everything every Secret Service agent had ever taught him during the long, boring nights in hotel suites and on campaign buses.

He managed to reverse their positions. He got in a good shot to Stefan's eye.

When the phone went skidding from Logan's hands, he lunged for it again – and that was his mistake.

Facedown in the mud, the cold seeped up from the ground and into Logan's bones. Stefan was on top of him and Logan couldn't breathe. Stefan was too heavy. And he had both hands on the back of Logan's head, pushing his face into the mud.

"This is what you are worth to me!"

Was Stefan yelling in Russian or in English? Logan didn't know. Didn't care. It was the last thing he was likely to ever hear in any case.

"This is what you are. I should kill you here. I should—"

"Why are boys so stupid?"

The voice was light and airy, like sunshine. And that's how Logan knew that he was dead – that even in death, Maddie Manchester was going to mock him, roll her eyes at him, taunt him until the end of time. It was the most comforting thought he'd had in ages.

But then Logan could breathe again – Stefan's weight was off his back, and Logan was able to roll over and look up into the freezing rain that struck his face like pinpricks, jolting him awake.

"You're alive," Stefan said, and Logan pushed away, gasping for air and grasping for balance as he pushed to his feet and turned to see the most beautiful sight he'd ever laid eyes on.

She must have washed the blood from her face, but a big bruise was growing at her temple. She was covered in mud and standing oddly, like she wanted to keep most of her weight on her right leg.

But Maddie was here. Maddie was alive.

"What are you doing?" Logan shouted.

"I couldn't let him kill you," she said, then smirked and looked at Stefan. "You see, I've been wanting to kill him for years. Couldn't let you steal my thunder."

"You lived," Stefan said, looking her up and down. Then Stefan actually smiled. "You must be very tough."

Maddie looked like she wanted to smirk again, but

Stefan went on. "And also very stupid."

Maddie shrugged at that. She actually looked like she might start chanting, *Sticks and stones may break my bones, but words from stupid Russian kidnappers can never hurt me.*

"I'm sure I am," she said. "But protecting *his* family happens to be my family business."

"Good." Stefan smiled. He reached down and pulled the satellite phone from the mud. He gathered up the map from where he'd dropped it. "This is very good."

Logan looked between the two of them as if maybe they had slipped into a language that he didn't speak.

"It's not good, Stefan," Logan told him. "If you haven't noticed, you're outnumbered."

Then Stefan turned on him, so fast it was like he wasn't frozen – wasn't tired, wasn't weary – at all. In the next moment, the knife was in his hand and at Logan's throat. When he spoke again, his mouth was an inch from Logan's ear.

"Oh, it is very good. Because now I have someone I can *kill*."

He pushed Logan towards Maddie and pulled the gun from the waistband of his jeans, pointed it in their direction while he went to retrieve his pack, sliding the phone inside.

Then he eased towards Maddie.

"Hands up."

Maddie complied, but not without saying, "OK. OK. But please … just don't judge me based on my cuticles,

OK? When your primary heating source is a wood-burning stove, dry skin is your perpetual enemy."

For a moment, Stefan looked at her like maybe she wasn't entirely sane, like maybe kidnapping the president's son and dragging him across the wilderness in the freezing rain was OK but maybe he had no idea what to do with any teenage girl who might willingly come along for the ride.

But he was so happy with his new, highly disposable hostage that he was willing to compromise whatever questionable code of honor he happened to have, Logan realized as Stefan dug a length of slender rope from his pack and wrapped it around Maddie's wrists, tighter and tighter. And then the truth sank in: Maddie wasn't just Logan's ally. She was also Stefan's hostage.

Once her wrists were bound, Stefan ran a hand down her side, and Logan wanted to kill the man, but for an entirely new reason.

"Don't touch her!" Logan shouted, but it was like he'd never said a word.

The only difference was that now Stefan was smiling as he felt along Maddie's leg. Her backside.

"Leave her alone!" Logan shouted, but Stefan pulled back and held a small pocketknife between two of his fingers after he pulled it from the back pocket of Maddie's jeans.

"This isn't much of a knife." He slid it into his own pocket as he laughed. "You won't survive for long out here with this, little girl," he said – and for the first time Maddie actually looked like this wasn't the best plan she'd ever had.

Had she actually expected him not to search her? Had she thought she was going to sneak up on Stefan and stab him with a knife that had a blade three inches long? Was that what Maddie was playing at?

Well, the game was up, Logan realized, and Stefan had moved on to Maddie's jacket.

When he pulled out a small tube of Vaseline, she cocked an eyebrow. "In Alaska, bears will totally kill you, but chapped lips will make you wish you were dead, so ..."

Stefan put the tube back in her pocket and didn't say a thing. He just ran his hands expertly down her arms and up her torso. When he reached the chain around her neck, Maddie looked affronted.

"Just because you're in the middle of nowhere doesn't mean a girl doesn't feel better when she's properly accessorized."

Which was more than Stefan could take. He looked more pained than when Logan had hit him as he pushed her away. "Enough!" Stefan shouted. "We walk now."

Stefan was readying the pack, taking one last look at the map. But Logan could only look at the face he'd thought he'd never see again.

"Why are you here? Why didn't you save yourself?" Logan asked. This time his voice actually broke. He was willing to die out here. He hadn't asked for this life, but he'd had seven years to get used to it – to accept the possibility.

But it should never have been Maddie's life, and the joy he'd felt when he found her bracelet was gone.

"Mad Dog, why didn't you run?" he asked again.

He honestly didn't expect an answer. He certainly wasn't expecting Maddie to raise her bound hands and throw them around his neck, to plaster her body against his and bring her lips to his mouth as if Logan might be holding her last breath.

He'd never kissed Maddie before. Until twenty-four hours ago, he'd never really thought about it. But he'd never cursed his handcuffs more than when he couldn't hold her, touch her, pull her close and keep her near and never, ever let her go.

Maddie hadn't run away – hadn't saved herself – because of this, Logan realized. This kiss.

He just didn't know how right he was until Maddie's lips parted and the kiss deepened … and Logan felt a small piece of metal pass from Maddie's mouth into his.

Then Maddie pulled back quickly.

She unwound her hands from around his neck, and when Stefan yelled, "Walk!" she did exactly as she was told.

Logan's legs weren't working right, though. Neither was his head.

Maddie had kissed him.

It was smart, he had to admit. How else could she be sure Stefan wouldn't find the key when he frisked her? What better way to pass Logan the key undetected?

She'd kissed him so that she could save him.

For the life of him, Logan had no idea why that made him feel so disappointed.

Chapter 13

Dear Logan,

OK, so I lied. I'm writing you another letter because, turns out, you're the only person I can really talk to. Even if you don't talk back. Maybe BECAUSE you don't talk back.

If you were here, you'd tell me that I do all the talking anyway. Then I'd point out that you saying otherwise totally negates your own point.

And then we'd probably argue about it for an hour. Maybe two. And then we'd go get ice cream.

So I'm gonna keep writing these letters.

I'm just never going to send them ever again.

Maddie

Maddie was real.

Maddie was alive.

Maddie was *here*.

And she was going to get them both killed.

"Oh my gosh! You guys walk so fast," she said, and for a moment she sounded almost like … Maddie. Or how Maddie used to sound when they were looking for ways to sneak into the Oval or trying to guess the middle names of all of the agents on his dad's detail. She sounded like Old Maddie. Not Older Maddie. Logan never realized how much he'd missed her.

He also never realized just how annoying she could be.

"I mean, it's no wonder you walk fast. Your legs are a lot longer than mine. How tall are you anyway?"

She turned around to look at Stefan, who had his gun out and pointed at her, but it didn't seem to faze Maddie. She just kept talking.

"You look tall. I'm only five four. I mean I pretend I'm five five, and I might be in boots. Do you think it counts if you're in boots?"

She stopped then and studied him. Stefan moved towards her and Logan jolted. He wanted to put himself between that gun and Maddie. And he wanted to put something between Maddie and the man.

"Who did you call?" Stefan snapped. "Who did you tell?"

Maddie actually scooted back, but she didn't look afraid. "What are you talking about?"

"Who did you call for help?" Stefan shouted – and this time Maddie looked at *him* like maybe *he* was crazy.

"No one. *There is no one here!*" She threw out her arms and spun around. "There's never anyone here."

Stefan didn't know Maddie like Logan did. Or like

Logan used to know her. He didn't hear the stress in her voice, didn't see the hurt in her eyes.

"No." Stefan shook his head. "You would not be so stupid as to get yourself captured."

"I don't know." Maddie shook her head. "I'm a teenage girl. People think we're pretty stupid."

Logan knew she was right. Logan also knew she didn't believe a word of it. Only a moron would, and Maddie was no moron. He'd seen enough in the barely twenty-four hours that he'd been here to know that Maddie had survived here – thrived here – for six years, almost entirely on her own. That Maddie was alive was proof enough that Stefan had absolutely no idea who he was dealing with.

That Maddie was smiling proved that she had every intention of keeping it that way.

"I thought I'd follow you, OK?" she went on. "I thought I might be useful."

Stefan looked at her for a long time, then let out a cold, clear laugh. "Useful how?"

Maddie shrugged. "I know things."

"I know things, too," Stefan said, all the laughter gone from his voice. "I know you're going to be very useful."

"I'm not going to let you kill him," Maddie said as if she had a choice in the matter – as if Stefan wasn't eight inches taller and sixty pounds heavier. As if he didn't have a gun and at least one knife and probably eight years of experience on her.

But the kind of experience Maddie had was different, and a part of Logan warmed at the thought.

"Where are my manners?" Logan tried to force as much sarcasm as possible into his voice. "Stefan, kidnapper extraordinaire, meet Maddie Manchester. Maddie, this is the man who tried to kill you."

"I *will* kill her if you get any ideas, Logan."

Logan gave a mocking smile. "You know my name. I'm touched."

"I can't touch you," Stefan stated. He sounded honestly disappointed, but then he turned to Maddie, pulled back his hand, and hit her hard across the face. Her head snapped and Logan actually heard the blow. He lunged for her, but halted, uncertain, as Maddie stumbled but managed to stay on her feet.

She didn't make a sound as Stefan finished, "But I *can* touch her."

"Leave her alone!" Logan yelled, but Stefan pulled Maddie close to him, a human shield.

His hand was around her throat, fingers not quite squeezing, but close. They could cut off her airway, crush her throat. They'd leave a bruise, Logan was certain, and it was just one more reason why he wanted his big, sharp rock back.

"I cannot hurt you, President's Son. But she has no value to me. Do we understand each other?" he asked, but Logan didn't answer. Words didn't come. "*Do we?*" Stefan shouted, the force of the words making his body shake and the hand at Maddie's throat tighten.

Maddie didn't make a single sound.

"Yes," Logan choked out.

"Good." Stefan took his arm away and pushed Maddie ahead of him. "Walk."

Maddie's throat didn't hurt. Not even a little bit. Her pride didn't either. Alaska never took it easy on her because she was a girl. Neither did her father. But ticked-off Russians probably didn't know that. By the look in Logan's eyes, neither did presidents' sons.

They both kept looking at her like she was just a … girl. Which was the best thing to happen to Maddie all day.

So she batted her eyelashes. She examined her nails. She didn't really talk again as they moved over the rough, wet ground.

Her hood was still up and pulled tight around her face. Maddie hated to lose her peripheral vision, but she wasn't going to be any help to anyone if she got sick. That was one lesson people in Alaska learned in a hurry.

"Are you OK?"

Maddie had to turn her head a little to look at Logan. She'd never seen him look like that – all stoic and broody and … hot.

She definitely wasn't going to think about how hot Logan looked because:

(A) It was Logan!

and

(B) She'd heard stories about girls who met cute boys and then lost their heads, and being that they were currently being held by a knife-wielding, ticked-off Russian, Maddie really didn't want to find out how literal that saying might be.

But Logan still looked worried – that much Maddie couldn't deny.

"It's going to be OK," she told him.

She kept her head down. She didn't turn again.

The rain was coming down more steadily, and it was possible that the man couldn't even hear her, so she risked a little more.

"They'll find us soon. Don't worry, Logan. Your team must have realized you were gone hours ago. You did a good job leaving a trail, and I left markers – really obvious markers. They'll find us soon."

Maddie was sure of it. She knew it in her gut. She'd lived her whole life with a man devoted to protecting others, and there were some things that all Secret Service agents had in common. They were all smart. And tough. And when they took a vow, they meant it. There was a reason that the Secret Service was the only arm of the US intelligence community that had never had a traitor.

Logan's detail was coming. And when they got there, Maddie only had to make sure she got Logan out of the way.

She turned her head. She smiled. She just wasn't expecting the look on Logan's face.

"They're not coming."

Logan's voice was low and he kept his head down, his gaze on the slick ground before them.

"Of course they're coming, Logan. They're good. I know those guys. Dad trained them."

"They're dead, Mad."

Maddie's steps actually faltered. There had been a little piece of her – a small sliver of light shining beneath the door of her mind, something telling her that hope was out there. Help was coming.

There had been a tiny voice whispering that she didn't have to do this alone.

She wasn't Logan's only chance.

She wasn't on her own – not really. She just had to keep Logan alive until the grown-ups came to take care of things.

But Maddie was the grown-up now, she knew, and she waited for the realization to hit her, for the panic to set in. But the panic didn't come, and Maddie didn't know whether to feel relief that she was prepared for this or sadness that being on her own was nothing new.

If Stefan had killed two Secret Service agents, then he wasn't just evil – he was also good at this. And Maddie didn't know which thought scared her more.

"Can your dad land in this?" Logan asked with a glance towards the sky that was growing darker, the rain that didn't feel like rain anymore. Maddie tipped her head up and felt the tiny stinging stabs that told her that sometime in the past five minutes the rain had turned to sleet.

Soon the ground would freeze, and the leaves and logs would be covered with ice and, eventually, snow.

"Mad, can your dad—" Logan started to repeat.

"I don't know," Maddie said. It was an honest answer. It also honestly scared her. "He won't take a chance. I made him promise that he wouldn't take any chances."

"Great." Logan kicked a rock, sent it tumbling down the hill.

Maddie knew exactly what it felt like.

"Help's gonna come, Logan," Maddie said. Maddie lied.

The weather was going to get worse and the night was going to be long, but the promise of help could be warmer than any fire, Maddie was certain.

"OK," Logan said. "But even if he does land in this, what's he gonna do? Drag himself through the woods to ... what? Find us?"

"Yes," Maddie said.

"He can't find us." Logan shook his head, but Maddie reached out and grabbed his arm.

They both had bound hands, but that just meant that both of her hands gripped both of his, like they were sharing some kind of solemn vow.

"I found you," she reminded him.

For a moment, Logan smiled. But then the smile faded. He shook his head and pulled away, started walking before Stefan could have an excuse or an opportunity to strike again.

"You should have run, Mad Dog."

"I did run. Right to you." She shrugged. "Someone has to keep you alive until help comes."

"Help's not coming."

Maddie knew better than to argue. So she tried a different angle. "Who is he?"

She didn't look back as she asked it. She just kept her head down, her face shielded against the sting of the falling ice.

"He's Russian," Logan said, as if that was all that mattered.

"You mean like …

Maddie didn't say *six years ago*. She didn't have to. That incident was never far from her mind, and it couldn't have been far from Logan's either. It had changed both of their lives in so many ways. Logan might have been the one who'd been grazed by a bullet, but she knew they both had scars.

"Yeah," Logan said. "Just like that."

"What else?" Maddie asked. She needed details, data. Before the president went anywhere, an advance team spent weeks going over an area with a fine-tooth comb. Facts mattered. Information mattered. And Maddie needed every speck of it that she could get.

"He's got a sat phone," Logan told her. "He's been speaking to someone. He doesn't know I can speak Russian."

"You can speak Russian!"

"Keep your voice down."

This time, Maddie whispered. "You can speak Russian?"

"Yes. I learned a lot in six years."

Maddie wanted to scoff and roll her eyes and yell at him and at the world, but she just kept walking. "Yeah. So did I."

When they passed a low bush covered with berries, Maddie said a silent prayer of thanks that the weather had been so wacky.

She pulled a bunch of berries off as quickly as she could and pushed them in Logan's direction.

"Here. Eat these." She helped herself to some as Logan eyed her.

"They could be poisonous."

Well, the berries weren't going to kill him, but Maddie's look could have, so he did as he was told.

"I don't know who he's working for," Logan admitted. The berries must have hit his bloodstream, a fresh shot of sugar and adrenaline and hope that lasted until Logan admitted, "And I don't know where he's taking me."

This time, Maddie smiled. "That's OK." She plopped a berry in her mouth. "I do."

Chapter 14

Dear Logan,

Someday I'm going to write a book: How Not to Die in Alaska – A Girl's Guide to Fashionable Survival.

I bet you don't know that a Kirby grip can make an excellent fishing hook. You may think you can use just any kind of mud for mud masks, but trust me, you CAN'T! In a pinch, nothing starts a fire like nail polish remover.

And don't even get me started on the lifesaving properties of a good pair of tights.

So I know a lot, in other words.

I just don't know why I'm still writing you these letters.

"I want you to get away."

At first, Maddie wasn't sure that Logan was talking to her. He could have been talking to himself, after all. He used to do that when they were kids. He'd mumble under his breath during tests at school or while they were eating snacks on the stairs or even while they huddled together in a tent on the lawn of the White House, pretending like they were on safari.

Maddie was used to the sound of Logan's voice, low and under his breath when he didn't think anyone was listening.

But Maddie was always listening.

"Maddie? Listen, I want you to get away."

"Shh," she warned, but she didn't look back at the man with the gun. And the knife. And the mysterious vendetta or cause.

"I'm going to undo the cuffs," Logan said. He gestured to the pocket where he'd placed the key. After the kiss.

Maddie absolutely did not let herself think about the kiss.

"He won't be expecting it. When I jump him, you can—"

"I'm not leaving you."

"You've got to leave me, Maddie." Logan risked a glance behind her. "He'll hurt you."

They couldn't stop.

It was getting too dark and the rain wasn't rain anymore. Ice was falling from the sky and collecting on the ground, covering fallen logs and the layer of leaves that blanketed the forest floor. Rocks were slick and sharp beneath their feet.

Maddie absolutely did not have time to stop and tell Logan he was an idiot.

But she really, really wanted to.

Mostly, she wanted him to feel as awful as she did.

"I've been hurt before, Logan. I'm getting pretty good at it."

But before she could turn and saunter off into the forest, point made, Logan took her hands in his. "They need me alive, Mad. They don't need you. They will hurt you."

"*You* need me," she said.

She watched the words wash over him, sink in. She saw how badly he wanted to shrug and argue, say that he didn't need a stupid girl to help him.

Which just showed how badly the opposite was true.

"You don't get it, Mad—" he said instead.

"No. *You* don't get it."

"Maddie—" Logan started, but Maddie was already turning around.

Shouting, "Mr. Kidnapper Man?"

She could practically hear Stefan's groan, but he still asked "What?"

"I need to go," she told him.

His gruff laugh cut through the air. "You're not going anywhere."

"No." Maddie crossed her legs. She bobbed up and down in the age-old way of two-year-olds everywhere. "I mean I need to *go* go."

Maddie never had the chance to learn Russian, but she knew a curse word when she heard one, no matter the language.

Loosely translated, it meant *girls are so annoying*.

On this, at least, he and Logan seemed to have found common ground.

"Fine," the man spat out after a moment. "We break."

They'd reached the side of the hill where the vegetation was thicker and the wind wasn't as strong. Maddie moved towards the thick bushes that were quickly turning white with ice.

"Stop!" the man yelled. Reluctantly, Maddie turned.

She actually rolled her eyes.

"Um … I'm mad at him" – she pointed at Logan – "and I don't know you, so I'm gonna need a little privacy."

The man looked at Logan again, as if he needed someone to explain stupid American females to him, but Logan only shrugged.

"Look," Maddie said, "I get it. You're a bad guy. You might not have any qualms about killing people, but I bet even you have the decency to let a sixteen-year-old girl pee in peace."

"Maddie …" Logan warned, but Maddie wasn't in the mood to listen.

Instead, she stepped closer to the man with the gun.

Stefan was strong. Athletic. Young. And he moved with such sure, easy grace that Maddie might have been impressed under any other circumstances. But these circumstances were far from normal.

In a flash, the knife was in his hand and he was moving towards her. Maddie saw Logan register the movement, but Stefan was too fast and too strong. When he grabbed her bound wrists and thrust the knife towards her, she didn't fight it. Even as Logan screamed "No!"

In the next moment Maddie's wrists were free. Blood was rushing back to her cold hands and they started to tingle and burn; she moved her fingers just to prove that she still could.

Logan, on the other hand, stood staring.

The man jerked his head towards the bushes and kept his knife on Logan.

"If you run, just remember: There are parts of him I do not need at all."

Pushing through the thick brush, Maddie heard her name. She spun back to look at Logan, who looked like maybe he'd never see her again.

"I'm not worth it," he told her.

She smiled. "I know."

Then she turned and pushed through the trees. Ice clung to branches, weighing them down and covering the forest in shiny, frosty sequins. It was like the whole world had been bedazzled, and Maddie could at least appreciate that aspect of it.

She was just starting to push aside a particularly shiny limb when something bolted out in front of her.

No.

Some*one*.

And Maddie didn't think about anything else.

She screamed.

When Logan heard the scream, he thought that it was over.

He just wasn't exactly sure what "it" was.

Maybe this long, terrible trek to an even more terrible fate. Maybe the fear that had been growing inside of him for hours.

But, no, Logan realized. What was over was the charade he was playing that Maddie wasn't the most important thing in the world to him right then – the idea that she hadn't been that for ages.

He didn't look at the man with the gun for permission. He didn't think about himself. He just burst through the dense trees and bushes, sliding over the slick ground, not caring about the ice.

It was a scream of shock and terror and it didn't matter to Logan what might happen to him. All he knew was that the bravest girl in the world sounded terrified.

And it was all his fault.

"Maddie!" he shouted, but he didn't hear anything back.

It was almost night, and the only light was that of a quickly fading dusk.

"Maddie!"

"It's OK."

When Logan heard her voice, he stopped and bent at the waist, hands on knees. He thought his heart might beat out of his chest.

"Maddie, where—"

"It's OK," a voice yelled. "It's just me."

The man who pushed through the brush wasn't as tall as the kidnapper, but he wore a thick coat and a wide-brimmed hat that kept the sleet at bay. He smiled at them, like maybe he'd been looking for them for hours.

But he hadn't. Logan could tell.

"Sorry to scare you folks. I just wasn't expecting to see anyone else out here. I can tell I'm not the only one."

Logan felt Stefan's eyes on him, saw the subtle shake of his head.

Then Logan noticed the firearm in a holster at the other man's waist.

"Which begs the question, what *are* you folks doing out here?" the man asked.

Logan saw Maddie standing just past the man's shoulder. He could actually see her thinking, planning.

"Nature hike," she said, and Logan felt Stefan coming up behind him. He felt the gun at his back.

"What are *you* doing here?" Stefan asked.

"Oh, just checking on things before the storm settles in and makes itself at home," the man said. He was dressed like a forest ranger. It made sense that some people would be posted in this vast wilderness, but Logan had never imagined they might cross paths with one.

"I think you folks are a long way from where you're supposed to be," the man said. "No one should be out here on a night like this."

There was some kind of war waging within Stefan – Logan could feel it.

Logan had pulled the sleeves of his jacket down to protect his freezing hands, and that, coupled with the dim and fading light, meant that the ranger probably had no idea that Logan's hands were bound. Maddie was running around, apparently free.

Did this man know that he'd just stumbled upon the kidnapping of the century? Had some kind of alarm been raised? Was every ranger within a hundred miles out looking for the first son right then?

Or was this simply sheer dumb luck?

"Are you lost?" The ranger looked right at Stefan. "Do you know what you're doing?"

"Yes," Stefan said. "I do."

But he wasn't talking about the route they were taking, the best tricks for staying warm and dry.

Stefan's voice had taken on an otherworldly quality as he said it, as if he'd been pulled back into some deep sleep.

Then he raised his gun.

He fired.

Once.

Twice.

And the ranger fell.

"No!" Maddie yelled, rushing towards the man. She clawed at his body, trying to turn him over, pull his face out of the ice and the mud. Trying to help him.

But he was too big and Maddie was too small, too cold. And Stefan was already there, ripping her away from the man and slinging her across the ice-covered floor of the woods.

She scampered back, crawling away. As if it were possible to escape, but whatever hope she might have had died when Stefan grabbed Maddie by the arm and jerked her to her feet.

When he pushed her towards Logan, she didn't say a word. She just threw her arms around Logan's waist and held him tight.

They held each other as if it might possibly be the last thing they'd ever do.

He didn't think a thing about it when she slid her hands beneath his jacket except to register that her hands felt warmer than they should, that they felt right. That maybe it was all worth it just to have this moment.

"I was so scared," he told her. "When you screamed, I ..."

But Logan trailed off when he felt her slide something beneath the waistband of his jeans at the small of his back, where the tail of his coat would hide it.

He pulled back and looked down into her eyes.

And he knew.

He risked a quick glance at the ranger's body on the ground.

The empty holster.

Logan wasn't sure whether he should be happy that they had a gun now or mad because this was almost as disappointing as the kiss.

Chapter 15

Dear Logan,

Remember when we were friends?

I do. But sometimes, honestly, I'd give anything to forget.

Maddie

The gun rubbed against the small of Logan's back with every step he took. It didn't scrape. It didn't hurt. It *burned*.

He'd never understood the phrase *burning a hole in your pocket* until then. He'd never known just how much self-restraint could hurt.

But his hands were bound in front of him, and he couldn't easily reach the gun without unclasping his cuffs. And Maddie had told him not to. In a way, she was far scarier than the very ticked-off Russian.

She wasn't even breathing hard as they climbed. Her footsteps never faltered, even once the ground was covered with sleet. Maddie knew that terrain.

But, most of all, Maddie had a plan.

If there was anything close to a home court advantage, she had it, and Logan tried to be smart. He tried to be patient.

He tried to forget the way Maddie had pressed against him, the feel of her hands at his back.

He tried to pretend like every single thing in his life wasn't changing. But Logan was smarter than anyone knew. Which meant that Logan knew that nothing in his life was ever going to be the same again.

"We have a gun," he whispered.

"Calm down, city boy. We have a *flare* gun, in case you didn't notice."

Logan hadn't noticed, but he wasn't as disappointed as he should have been. Right then, the *gun* part was the only part that mattered.

But Maddie wasn't so sure. "This means one shot. One shot means we have to be smart about it."

"Maddie—"

"Listen to me, Logan. Listen now. You have to do what I tell you. When I say something you can't ask *what*. You can't ask *why*. You can't argue. And for the love of all that is holy, you *cannot* try some stupid macho move that is only going to get us both killed. OK? You have to *listen* to me."

"OK," he said, partly to make her stop talking. Stefan was close, and even though it was dark and the sleet was falling harder, it was so quiet out there that even a whisper seemed to echo for an hour.

"No. Logan, listen to me. You have to do *exactly* what I say *exactly* when I say it. Promise me."

"I promise," he said, and she nodded like maybe – just maybe – she might be in the mood to believe him.

She put her head down and kept trudging through the storm, and for a moment Logan thought that maybe everything was going to be OK, but then Maddie stumbled to a stop. When she spun, there was terror in her eyes.

"No!" she screamed.

Behind them, Stefan kept walking. He nudged her forward. "We do not stop here."

But Maddie was shaking her head, shouting, "I know where you're taking us."

"You know what I need you to know."

"I know that map is about twenty years out of date." She pointed at the folded pieces of plastic-covered paper sticking out from the pocket of his pack.

"Walk," he ordered.

"No."

"Mad—" Logan tried, but she pulled away from him and kept glaring up at Stefan, a look of rage – or maybe fear – in her eyes.

"If you think we're going to cross it, you're crazy. Or you have a death wish. Or both."

"Mad?" Logan had no idea what she was talking about, but Maddie was too frantic to fill him in.

"You're crazy!" she shouted. "We should go to Black

Bear Bridge. I mean, it's not a bridge made of black bears, don't worry. But it's about twenty years newer and a hundred times safer – and if you haven't already noticed, we're not exactly dealing with ideal conditions here."

"What are you talking about?" Logan snapped. He was hungry and he was cold and frustration was coming off of him in waves.

But Maddie kept her gaze locked on Stefan. "Look, I know you don't care about me. And you probably don't even care about yourself. I get that. But you care about *him*." She pointed at Logan. "And he's not going to do you any good if he's at the bottom of a hundred-foot ravine, smashed into about a million little icy pieces." That part at least seemed to hit its mark. "I don't want to die. And you need him alive. So please. Let's just go to Black Bear Bridge."

Logan watched Stefan consider this. "How far is this Black Bear Bridge?" the Russian asked.

"It's not too far."

"How far?" Stefan snapped.

Maddie couldn't meet his gaze. "It's only a half day's walk."

"A half day's walk?" Stefan asked. "Under good conditions?"

Maddie had to nod.

"We go my way," Stefan said, and pushed forward.

"Let her go back," Logan was still pleading with Stefan ten minutes later. "It'll take her a day to walk back to her cabin, and you and I will be long gone by then, won't we? I mean, that's why we can't go to this other bridge, right? Because we're on a deadline here? Then let her go. You don't need her."

"Yes. I do."

Some faces just weren't supposed to smile. Stefan's was one of them, Maddie decided. Because when he grinned at Logan's words, it had an eerie effect, like he was ten moves away from checkmate and he was the only one who could see it. It made Maddie's heart pound harder, her hands want to shake. She wanted to reach for her own rock and take her chances, but that wasn't the smart play.

And they were currently in the middle of almost twenty million acres of wilderness with heavy precipitation and falling temperatures and absolutely no help on the way.

They didn't have time for stupid.

But that didn't wipe the smile from Stefan's face. It didn't dampen the fire that was burning inside of Logan.

"What's so funny?" Logan snapped. "Just let her go!"

It might have been sweet. Or heroic. Or even romantic – if Stefan hadn't taken a few more steps and then turned on them. The hill was tall and steep. Landslides and glaciers had scraped away huge chunks where no trees grew and the snow and the rain didn't stick. A river ran beneath them, curving through the forest like a snake. Freezing rain kept falling and the water down below was from the melting glaciers, which meant even in the middle of summer it was cold.

In good conditions, with the right gear, a person could climb down there. Maybe wade across if he had a death wish. But that would take time ... and time was one of many things they didn't have.

And that's what brought them here – to a tenuous lifeline that ran between this hill and the next. Even in the darkness and the sleet it practically glowed, probably because it was covered with ice and looked like something that a Disney princess might have summoned and built with her two hands. In the remaining traces of light it practically glistened, shining like crystals. But Maddie knew what lay underneath.

Ropes ran across the gorge. Wooden planks had once been placed at regular intervals, spanning the two hundred feet of the bridge. But there had been too much rain, too much snow. Too many hot summer days and strong mountain winds in the twenty or so years since anyone stopped caring. No one ever came here. No one who did come here would forget that there was another, safer bridge not too terribly far away.

No one would be stupid enough to cross.

"I need your girlfriend, President's Son," Stefan said. "I need her to go across that bridge and show us how safe it is."

Safe wasn't a word that had been used to describe it in over a decade. Maybe longer. Long before she and her father had moved to Alaska. She had heard about this bridge, about how the parks department meant to come tear it down every summer, but with cutbacks and budget freezes it got delayed every year. Besides, it's not like anyone ever came here. It's not like anyone would ever be stupid enough – desperate enough – to try to cross it.

"She's not going across that," Logan said. He positioned his large body in between Maddie and Stefan.

"Logan?" Maddie's voice was smaller than it should have been.

"She's not doing it! She's not some kind of puppet. She's—"

"Logan?" Maddie tried again, but he was staring daggers into Stefan.

"We need you alive," Stefan reminded Logan. "So the girl can go or the girl can die here."

Stefan pulled his gun from his waistband and pointed it in Maddie's direction, but Logan was already shielding her.

Like he cared.

He just hadn't cared enough to write.

"Move," Stefan ordered.

"Logan?"

"You're not going to hurt her!" Logan shouted.

But Maddie just threw up her hands. "Boys!"

Logan seemed to remember exactly who was behind him. That she was a real person with a voice and opinions. She wasn't some ideal.

"Logan, listen to me." She grabbed him by the collar and pulled him close. Luckily Stefan had never retied her hands, so she was able to wrap her arms around him, feel him one more time.

"I'll be OK," she said.

"No, Mad. You can't do this."

But that was exactly the wrong thing to say because she pulled back. She actually cocked an eyebrow. "Watch me."

Logan wasn't willing to let her go. He took her arm. "No, Mad. I'm not going to let you."

"You're not *letting* me," she said, but when Logan dragged her closer she didn't fight. She didn't squirm or scream or push him away. No. That might have tipped Stefan off to exactly how formidable she was.

Yes. Exactly. That had to be why Maddie didn't resist at all when Logan pulled her body right up against his and said, "I'm not going to lose you again."

He even sounded like he meant it.

He looked into her eyes. "That's not a bridge, Mad Dog. It's suicide."

"Do you trust me?" Maddie asked.

"Hurry up!" Stefan yelled.

"Logan, do you trust me?" she asked again, urgent now. Time was running out. In a lot of ways.

And Logan nodded.

So Maddie went up on her tiptoes and pressed a warm kiss to Logan's cold cheek.

Then she whispered in his ear, "Step *exactly* where I step. And be *ready*."

She could see the question in his eyes: *Ready for what?* But he was at least smart enough not to say it aloud. Instead, he seemed to hold his breath.

And watch.

The ground at the mouth of the bridge was flat and wide and, by that point, covered with at least an inch of ice and snow. It actually crunched beneath Maddie's feet, tiny ice pellets grinding into almost nothing, pressing hard against the ground and getting slicker with every moment. Surely that was why she took a huge step, an awkward lunging jump that seemed to bypass as much of that space in front of the bridge as possible. But she was steady and sure on her feet as she eased towards the posts that stuck up from the ground. She reached out for them and pulled, relieved when they didn't wiggle. Then she gave one last look back.

"Logan?"

"You don't have to do it, Mad Dog," he said again, but she shook her head.

"Did you get my letters?" Maybe she was a fool for stepping out onto that bridge, but she couldn't do it without knowing. Once and for all.

He shook his head. "What letters?"

And then it was Maddie's turn to smile, but it was one without joy.

"I'll see you on the other side," she said.

When Maddie took a step, the first board was so slick that she actually skidded. There wasn't any traction, and Maddie had to grip the braces at the mouth of the bridge to steady herself. She almost fell to her knees.

"Maddie!" Logan yelled and lunged forward, but she looked back and shook him off.

"I'm fine," she said. "Just … *exactly*." She mouthed the last word and stared into his eyes, willing him to hear her, see her. Believe her, knowing that for the first time in her life someone needed to follow in her footsteps.

When she was steady on her feet again, she tried the next board. And the next.

The third one creaked, but it seemed steady enough, so Maddie risked shifting her weight, only to have it splinter beneath her. But her hold on the rope handles held.

The old rope was freezing. As she moved her hand, ice slid off of the coarse bristles and bit into her cold skin. She was like a tiny, one-woman snowplow, clearing the way.

One step. Then another. Some of the boards were missing. Others hung at odd angles, and with the ice she didn't trust herself not to slip and fall. Only once did she have to jump, but Maddie was part goat, her father always said, and she landed lightly on the other side.

She risked a glance back at Logan.

"It's solid," she yelled. She might have even meant it.

But Logan was shaking his head. "Maddie, come back."

"Keep going!" Stefan shouted. His gun was out and pointed at Logan's back.

"Logan, come on," Maddie called to him.

"Mad—"

"Logan, you have to trust me. Please."

Maybe it was the *please* that did it. But he took one last look at Stefan, then moved towards the bridge.

Chapter 16

Dear Logan,

Forgive me for not writing for several days. You see, I've been extremely busy with my new, oh-so-exciting life. See?

Things to do in Alaska:

– chop wood

– catch fish

– clean fish

– haul wood

– catch some more fish

– try not to get eaten, smashed, burned, poisoned, or just, in general, die

Seriously, trying not to die in Alaska is kind of a full-time job.

Maddie

Logan stared at where Maddie stood, in the center of a bridge that looked like it should have already fallen based on the weight of the snow and the ice alone. Much less with Maddie's weight. Much less with his.

"Logan, it's OK!" she called to him. "Just do what I said."

He heard her words again: *From this moment on, step exactly where I step.*

There were things the Secret Service agents had to teach him, back when he was a kid and his dad was just a candidate – back when no one assumed they knew him. Back when Maddie really did.

The first lesson they teach a protectee is that, if an agent says duck, you duck. If an agent says run, you run. You don't stop for questions. You never, ever say *What?* Because in the time it takes you to stop and say that single word, a sniper can strike from a thousand yards away. It's the protectee's job to follow directions and then get out of the way and let the professionals do their jobs.

Maybe it was that training coming back to him. Or maybe it was the look in Maddie's eyes when she asked Logan to trust her. Logan swore right then that he never wanted to disappoint Maddie ever again. He owed her that much at least. He was going to mirror her movements exactly, even if he was at least fifty pounds heavier than she was. In the part of his brain that was always thinking, analyzing, calculating, Logan knew that just because a board was strong enough to hold her there was no guarantee that it would be strong enough to hold *him*. But it was as good a place as any to start.

He inched towards the bridge and paused to look down

at the icy ground in front of him. It had been blowing and swirling all day and something like a drift covered the mouth of the bridge. But it wasn't so deep he had to wade.

"Remember! Be careful," she shouted. And something in Logan knew – just knew – that it was the *remember* that mattered.

Be ready, she'd said.

But ready for what?

There was only one way to find out.

Logan's footprints dwarfed Maddie's as he stepped into her tracks and moved slowly towards the bridge.

He could still feel Stefan behind him, on Logan's right, where he had an angle on both of his captives. Stefan kept the gun trained on Logan as he matched Maddie's big step onto the mouth of the bridge, mirroring her in every way. But Logan's hands were still cuffed in front of him, and he could only hang on to one side.

When he slipped on a slick board it was harder than it should have been to catch himself. His body kept twisting at the waist to grip the rope handles and he couldn't get centered.

When Logan slipped again, he risked a glance at Stefan, a smirk. "Bet you're wishing you hadn't thrown away that handcuff key about now, aren't you?" he asked.

"Walk!" Stefan ordered, and Logan forced himself to turn around.

Maddie was still inching closer to the other side, but

she turned to him and nodded slowly, the universal signal for *it's time*.

So, slowly, Logan reached into his pocket for the key Stefan had thrown away that morning. In the darkness, Stefan couldn't see well enough to know what Logan was doing when he unhooked the left wrist cuff but kept his hands together.

With a glance back, he could see that Stefan had put away his gun and was approaching the bridge himself.

Maybe it was because he was coming from a slightly different angle. Maybe it was because he didn't think he had to listen to a teenage girl. Or maybe it was common sense for him to step right up to the edge, to the place where bridge met land. To the place where the snow was a little bit thicker.

To the place that Maddie – and then Logan – had jumped right over.

Stefan stepped into the deep snow and immediately his foot disappeared.

For a moment nothing happened.

And then Logan heard the snap.

The yell.

A moment later Stefan was falling over and digging at the snow and ice, pulling at his leg. But it wasn't just his leg.

Something clung to Stefan's dark jeans, like an animal that had locked its jaws around his calf and was hanging on for dear life. But it wasn't an animal, Logan realized.

No. In that moment *Stefan* was the animal, as he pried the metal jaws apart and pulled his leg free of the trap.

"Logan, run!" Maddie yelled, and Logan realized that she'd already made it to the far side of the bridge.

This was her plan.

This was their chance.

But Stefan had already pried the trap off his leg and tossed it into the abyss below. Hate and rage radiated from him.

They didn't have a moment to lose.

Stefan must have been so angry that he ignored Maddie's footsteps and started to run. As soon as his big foot landed on the first rung of the bridge, the board snapped. The bridge jerked beneath Logan's feet as Stefan grabbed at the ropes and lunged forward. The next board snapped, too, and Logan knew it was no accident.

He thought about the small knife that Stefan had taken from Maddie, and just like that he knew. Maddie had come here. Maddie had done this.

He had to get to Maddie.

Now.

Stefan's strong arm was wrapped around the icy ropes of the bridge. His good leg dangled down between the broken slats. There was too much pressure on the leg that had been in the trap. When he screamed, it sounded like a bear had been caught in Maddie's trap instead of a man.

And Logan didn't dare stick around to see if his bite was as bad as his growl.

"Logan, *exactly*!" Maddie yelled again, and Logan tried to match his steps to hers.

He tried to be fast.

He tried to be careful.

He needed so badly to be with Maddie again, both of them finally on the same side of the river after what felt like a lifetime apart.

Stefan grappled behind him, and the ropes swung. The bridge shifted, snow and ice crashing off the sides and disappearing into the vast darkness below.

But he was almost there. He could actually make out the look in her eyes – the little ring of blue that surrounded her irises. It was dark and he knew he couldn't actually see it – not really. But he could see her in a way he hadn't in years.

Somehow, it was a way he had *never* seen her.

So when the look of terror filled her eyes, he couldn't help but turn back.

Stefan had dragged himself free of the broken boards and was on his feet again, running towards them.

"Logan, now!" Maddie shouted, and Logan leaped towards her, bypassing the last six steps of the bridge. He landed hard on the ground and rolled as Maddie reached for him.

He tried to get to his feet. They had to run. They had to—

But Maddie's arms were around him then, pulling something from the small of his back.

She got free and rolled. Then, in one single, fluid motion she cocked the flare gun and aimed at the center of the old rope bridge.

There was still ice all over it, but Maddie had scraped away a lot as she walked, and when she took aim there was no indecision, no crisis of conscience or faith.

She was the image of her father as she fired.

Logan hadn't realized how dark it had gotten – it had happened little by little, bit by bit. But as soon as the flare left the gun it was instantly daylight – if sunlight were the color of fire.

Red streaked across the sky and soared across the dark ravine.

It reminded Logan vaguely of the Fourth of July. The first year he'd celebrated at the White House, Maddie had come over and her dad had made arrangements for them to go up on the roof with the snipers. It was the best view in DC, everyone said, and they'd lain together on an itchy blanket watching fireworks over the Washington Monument. Logan remembered the big, booming sounds, the streaking lights in reds and blues. But most of all, he remembered thinking that he should hold Maddie's hand but knowing that would be weird since she'd just started being his friend. His only friend. He couldn't run the risk of grossing her out by touching her with the hand he'd been using to eat popcorn with too much butter.

And that's what he thought about then.

Not Stefan.

Not Alaska.

Not even how cold and hungry and exhausted he was. How terrified.

Logan just wished he'd been brave enough to hold Maddie's hand.

When the flare hit the center of the bridge, nothing happened for a moment. It seemed as if maybe the fire was going to die there, smothered by the snow and the ice.

But then the old ropes and wood exploded in a wave of color and fire and heat, and Logan didn't doubt anymore. He swore to never put off anything ever again, and he reached for Maddie's hand, pulled it into his own.

It was so small, and not nearly as smooth as it should have been. It was a hand that had known work and hardship and ...

Maddie pulled away, and Logan fought the hurt that was growing in his chest. Maybe she didn't want to touch him. Maybe she really did hate him, would hate him forever.

But Maddie walked to the side of the bridge, and then he saw a huge knife buried in the post, waiting.

"Stefan took your knife," he blurted like an idiot.

Maddie looked like she'd never been more insulted in her life. "I never leave the house with just one knife. Seriously. Do I look like a one-knife kind of girl?" She pulled it from the post and Logan could see the fire glistening off of a long blade that could have easily sliced through those old ropes. But they hadn't needed it. Yet.

She shoved the knife into a sheath in her boot. "Always have a backup," she said, and Logan heard a crack. He looked back to see the bridge breaking apart.

Stefan had rushed back to the other side, but he'd lost his pack. It was lying there, in the center of the bridge that was burning all around him.

The pack with the satellite phone.

Logan didn't think. He just started for the bridge. If he could get the pack, he could get the phone, and then this would all be over.

The pack was between Logan and the fire and he could get there. He could—

But he never made it to the bridge, because Maddie's hand was back in his again, holding tight, yanking in the opposite direction.

"I can get it!" he yelled, but Maddie pulled back.

"Leave it!" she shouted.

Smoke filled the air as the fire spread. In the new light he could see her plainly, the worry in her eyes. The tension and the fear.

He tried to pull away again.

"We need it!" he shouted, but Maddie was stronger than she looked. So very strong as she pulled him back to her, wrapped her arms around his waist, and held him tight.

"I need you more."

The fire crackled and the bridge burned, and Logan

knew without a shadow of a doubt that they could never, ever go back. This moment was going to change their lives forever.

He turned and looked at what lay on this side of the ravine. More trees. Another steep hill and ice-covered rocks.

And then he heard it, something like a pop. He risked a glance back, expecting to see the bridge finally breaking apart and falling into the abyss, but the bridge still stood. Barely.

He heard the sound again, the echo of the shot off the steep stone walls of the mountains that surrounded them. And through the smoke and the haze and the falling snow he saw the assassin on the opposite bank, arm raised and steady. Stefan's gun didn't even quiver as he shot again. And again.

"Run!" Logan and Maddie both shouted, and they started for the cover of the trees.

They never stopped holding hands.

Chapter 17

Dear Logan,

The next time you see me, you should call me Dr Maddie. I basically have a medical degree in first aid. I mean, I know there is no such thing, but there totally should be. I can dig out a splinter using a safety pin or a pair of tweezers (which, really, what self-respecting girl DOESN'T have a pair of tweezers?). I can treat burns and scrapes and lots of stuff way too gross to put on paper.

So, yeah. Call me Dr Maddie.

But who am I kidding?

You're never going to call me anything ever again.

Maddie

Logan could hear the shots still coming, long after he and Maddie were lost among the cover of the trees. The red glow of the fire was fading, but they took advantage of what light there was. Soon, there would be nothing but darkness and more snow. And probably bears.

Man, he really hoped there wouldn't be bears.

But then an even scarier thought occurred to him.

"Mad, is there really a Black Bear Bridge?"

She looked up at him. "Yes."

He wanted to curse but didn't. "I saw it on the map, I think. But it didn't look like a half day's walk."

"No. It's closer. But he doesn't know that. And I needed him to come this way. I needed …" She trailed off. She was breathing hard, Logan noticed. She'd been so strong for so long. He wanted to hug her, but the hand-holding was new enough. He didn't want to risk it.

"It worked, Mad. It was genius. It was evil. You're an evil genius, and I'm … I'm glad you're on my side."

"Don't act so surprised," she told him.

They walked on for a few minutes. The light of the fire was almost gone now. They couldn't even hear the Russian curse words piercing the too-cold, too-clear air.

With every step the snow and sleet fell harder, collecting on their hoods and their shoulders, and Logan didn't want to think about what would happen if they stopped moving, even for a minute.

"What's over here?" he asked.

"On this side of the river?"

"Yeah. There wasn't much detail on Stefan's map."

As Maddie shrugged, she lost her footing for a moment. She held tighter to Logan's hand to keep her feet.

"More of the same, I think," she said. "A few mining roads that have been out of commission for ages. An old ranger's station, but no one uses it, and I doubt it's stocked. Plus, it'd take all day to walk there."

Logan looked around the dark forest. "We're running out of day."

"Yes," Maddie said, and Logan could actually hear her teeth chattering.

"You're freezing," he said, trying to pull her closer.

Maddie winced and pulled away.

At first, he felt silly. He felt hurt. Maybe the hand-holding and the kissing and the superdramatic hugging were all for Stefan's benefit. Maddie was never going to have to slip a key from her mouth into his again, he realized. He was almost disappointed.

But then Maddie stumbled on the almost smooth ground. She was no longer the girl who had leaped across a decaying, ice-covered bridge. Instead, she was bending at the waist, and even in the darkness, Logan could tell that her face was too pale. Her hand had been too cold – even given the air and the snow and the terrible day they'd had.

"I'm fine. It's just a scratch," she said, but the words slurred and she swayed again.

"Maddie!" he snapped. He was almost mad at her. He was furious at himself as he went for the zipper of her outer jacket. She tried to push his hands away, but she was too weak.

His heart pounded in his chest and his hands started to shake for reasons that had nothing to do with the cold as he unzipped her jacket. Then he pulled aside a layer and felt it – something warm and sticky beneath the logo on her jacket.

Something that smelled like blood.

Maddie swayed a little. She tried to laugh as she looked up into his eyes and said, "Tag. I'm it."

And then she passed out cold.

Maddie was dreaming. She had to be. Why else would it feel like she was flying, floating through the air? Why else would she be hearing Logan's voice, talking to her through the dark?

"Stay with me, Mad Dog. I've got you. You're gonna be OK. Wake up, Maddie. Wake up. Wake up!" Logan shouted.

But it wasn't Logan. It couldn't be. Logan was back in DC and he wasn't her friend anymore. He'd never be her friend again.

Logan had died in that White House corridor. Her friend had died, gone away forever. But now he'd come back to her.

In her dream.

Maddie tried to roll over. She wanted to pull the covers up higher, wrap herself in them tighter. She wanted to stop shaking.

"No. Don't. Stop fighting, Mad Dog," Dream Logan

told her, but Maddie wanted to laugh at him. Shows what he knew.

Maddie never could stop fighting.

But first she had to get warm.

She really should get up and put some more wood on the fire, but her eyelids were too heavy. And Dream Logan, as annoying as he might be, was better than No Logan. So Maddie let her eyes stay closed.

"Here," Dream Logan told her, and Maddie was suddenly warmer.

Maddie was so warm. She felt so safe. And so she slept.

And she had dreams of Real Logan, even though he was a lifetime away.

Chapter 18

Dear Logan,

I'm sorry that the stupid Russians shot you.

Mainly because I really want to shoot you, and I hate that they beat me to it.

Maddie

Maddie wasn't dying.

No. Logan wouldn't let her.

When he was little, Logan's mother used to tell him that he was the most stubborn child in the world. But that had been before they'd both met Maddie. She never gave up. She never gave in.

Maddie clung to life, so Logan clung to her. The farther he walked, the tighter he held her, and Logan didn't even feel the chill of the falling snow, even though he'd wrapped her in his jacket. He could still see the traces of blood on her face from her fall this morning. He knew the wound on her shoulder was probably still bleeding no matter how hard he had tried to stop it.

The little strip of red made him think about DC and *That Night*, about the fluttering fabric that trailed behind the rolling cart, about the realization that he might be about to lose his mother.

And then Logan realized that was no longer the scariest moment of his life.

This was the scariest moment of his life.

So Logan gripped her harder and kept moving.

Away from the burning bridge. Away from Stefan's only path over the ravine, assuming he made it there through the storm and the darkness.

Logan wasn't going to let Maddie go. Not now. Not ever again.

As soon as he stepped out of the helicopter – as soon as he'd seen her – he'd known she was different. Not just taller. Not just stronger. Not just significantly less sparkly.

No, the real change in Maddie had been in her eyes. They'd always shone like maybe they were bedazzled. But that light was gone, Logan had thought the day before.

Was it just a day?

He had to think. Of course it was. He'd been in Alaska a little over twenty-four hours.

He looked down at the girl who was sleeping in his arms. For twenty-four hours she had felt like a stranger, but with her eyes closed, in the shadowy darkness of the forest with only the palest hint of moonlight reflected off the snow, she looked like the Maddie he used to know, like maybe she had fallen asleep watching a movie or maybe like she was just playing, wanting him to tickle her awake. For a minute, he could see his Maddie in the girl in his arms, as long as she was asleep.

So it was harder than it should have been to shake her one more time and say, "Maddie, wake up."

But she didn't even stir.

And Logan knew whatever he was doing, it wasn't enough.

He eased her to the ground and held his breath as he felt for her pulse. It was there, but faint. He leaned closer and felt her breath on his cheek – too light, though. He could see his own breath fogging in the cold air, but Maddie's was invisible. He had to check again, to make sure it was there.

And only then did Logan start to feel himself panic.

He'd read books on first aid. He'd gone through a documentary kick two summers before, and he knew that Maddie had lost a lot of blood today. She'd been shot. She'd been knocked down a cliff. And head wounds bled like crazy. Plus she was so little and it was so cold outside. No wonder she was shaking.

Except …

Logan went from scared to terrified when he realized she was no longer shaking.

"Maddie!" he yelled. He had to get her awake. He had to get her warm. He had to get her dry and hydrated and fed and … safe. He had to get Maddie safe.

But the snow was heavier. It landed on her face with thick white flakes that melted on her smooth skin. It made it look like she was crying.

And now that Logan had stopped walking, he was starting to shiver, too. His skin was actually slick with sweat, but that was a lie. Logan wasn't hot. His body was lying to his mind, and soon the shock of it all was going to set in. Soon he was going to crash from this adrenaline and then …

Logan wasn't going to think about what happened then.

He rested for a moment, sitting on a log, but he kept Maddie on his lap. Maybe to consolidate their body heat. Maybe he didn't want to place her frail body on top of the snow and the ice. Or maybe Logan just wasn't going to let her go again. Ever. So he kept her on his lap as he thought.

"Hey, Mad Dog."

Somehow, Logan knew he had to keep talking. Not for her. But for him.

"You got big, you know. But I guess I got bigger. Mom told me to stop growing, but it's been a long time since I've done what they told me to do. You know that, don't you?"

Logan looked up at the sky that was so dark. He'd never seen anything so dark. He'd lived most of his life in cities, and even in the country – at places like Camp David – in Logan's world there were security lights and headlights and flashlights.

There was always light.

But Logan and Maddie were alone in the darkness. He knew that there were millions of acres around them, and Logan didn't see a single, solitary light – not on any of the distant hills. They were very much alone.

"I don't think your dad's going to be able to make it back in this, Mad Dog." He touched her forehead. It was still warm, but not too warm. If a fever was coming, it hadn't found her yet.

"I think you're stuck with me. I think we're alone. But that's OK. I promise not to tell anyone. I don't think they'll make us get married."

He looked down at her sleeping face.

Sleeping, Logan reminded himself. He absolutely refused to even think the word *unconscious*.

"That was a joke, Mad Dog. Wake up and laugh. Or, better yet, wake up and call me an idiot. Do it, I dare you."

Maddie never had been able to turn down a dare.

That must have been what did it, because Logan saw the snowflakes on her long, dark eyelashes start to flutter.

"Logan," she said, then tried to move. She tried to roll over in his arms, but Logan just held tighter.

"You're not here," she said, eyelids fluttering again, then going still, like she wanted to go back to sleep, but Logan couldn't let that happen.

"Maddie, stay with me."

"You're not here," she said again, but he shook her. Gently.

"Oh, I'm not?" He wanted to laugh, he was so happy just to hear her groggy words.

She tried to twist in his arms again, but this time she was twisting closer, snuggling into his warmth, and Logan didn't fight her in the least.

"No. You're gone," she said. "I'm just dreaming that you're here. And that you're hot now."

"You think I'm hot?"

Maddie made a little sound and nodded, something like *uh-huh*. "Dream You is. But he's not real."

She sounded sad. Disappointed. Lonely.

Logan looked out over the vast, empty darkness. Of course she was lonely. She'd been alone out here long before they were alone out here together.

"Maddie, I'm real," he whispered, and ran a finger across her forehead, tucking a stray hair underneath the shelter of her tightly drawn hood.

"No," she said. "You died."

Then Maddie drew a deep breath and shuddered, wincing in pain. When she closed her eyes, he could almost feel her start to slip away again.

"No! No, stay with me, Maddie. Mad Dog! Wake up!"

Logan was screaming, but he no longer cared who heard him.

"Stay with me, Mad Dog," he tried again. He shifted her in his arms like a baby who is trying to learn to sit up. "Maddie!"

"Logan?" she said, and she sounded a little more like

herself. Which meant she sounded a little like she hated him. It was the sweetest sound that he had ever heard.

"Where's your coat?" she asked.

"You're wearing it," he told her. He didn't even try to hide his smile.

"You're an idiot," she said, trying to push herself upright, trying to take his coat off, he could tell, and give it back to him. But as soon as she moved, she winced. He could see the pain on her face, hear it in her voice as she cried out.

"No, Maddie. Don't move. You're hurt."

"Logan ..." He could tell she wanted to argue. Even frozen and bleeding and half dead, Maddie wanted to argue. Then she remembered. "I was shot."

"Yes," he said, then tried to smile. "Your shoulder hurts, I know."

Maddie nodded as if remembering. He *did* know.

"How long was I out?"

"An hour? Maybe less. Probably less. But it felt like forever. I carried you away from the bridge and – Maddie, stay still. I've got you." He adjusted his grip on her, even though he knew he should get up. They had to keep moving. The sweat was drying on his body, and soon he would start shaking. He couldn't let that happen. He had to get her to safety or, at the very least, get her warm.

"We can't stay here, Logan," she said as if reading his mind. "We're sitting ducks here."

"He's on the other side of the river, remember?"

But Maddie had finally pushed herself upright. She had to face him. "That man's not the most dangerous thing in Alaska."

Five minutes before, Logan had been certain he'd never been more afraid in his life, but something in Maddie's voice changed all that. She knew what she was talking about. She'd survived here for years. And the way she was pushing herself off his lap, the urgency with which she pulled off his coat and her own told him that this mattered. So he didn't argue.

"There were berries," she said.

"Yes. Do you want me to find some. I can ..."

But Logan trailed off when Maddie started stripping. He knew he should have argued, but he'd lost the ability to speak at all.

It was well below freezing, but Maddie didn't stop. She just peeled off layer after layer until she could see the piece of Logan's T-shirt that he had shoved inside her clothes in hopes of stopping the bleeding.

She turned her back to him.

"Is there an exit wound?" she asked.

Numbly, Logan nodded.

"Is there?" she snapped, and he realized she couldn't see him well.

"Yes."

"Good."

"Get some snow. We have to wash the blood off."

"Maddie, I don't care about a little blood. I care

that you're going to freeze to death."

"It smells," she said.

"I don't care that you stink, Mad."

"The bears are awake, Logan," she practically snapped. "There were berries today, remember? Which means they haven't run out of food yet. They should have started hibernating by now, but the climate is all screwed up and winters are so much shorter and ... the bears are awake. Did you know bears have one of the best senses of smell of any predator on the planet? Polar bears can follow a scent for thirty miles. Grizzlies and black bears are almost as good, and we are surrounded by grizzly and black bears. Now help me wash the blood off."

"They could be hibernating," he told her.

It took a beat for her to answer. And it scared him.

"They're not," was all she said.

"But—"

"I saw one. Earlier today. When I was following you guys. I had to be quiet, which violates rule one of life in Alaska: You always want a bear to hear you coming. But I couldn't let you guys hear me coming, so ... I saw one."

"Are you OK?" he asked.

She pushed his worry away. "I'm fine. He wasn't interested in me. But now that the weather's turned ..."

"Oh," Logan said.

Maddie looked at him. "You think I stink?"

"No. I ... Let's get you cleaned up."

Maddie reached down, pulled the knife from her boot, and started cutting away the pieces of her shirt that were the bloodiest.

Even in the moonlight, Logan could tell that Maddie's skin was as white as the snow. He might have called her Snow White. He might have joked or teased, but she was starting to shake again. He could tell she was struggling to stay upright.

But the bullet had passed right through her shoulder, and the wound was clotting well. They tore up her base layer and used it to scrub away the blood as best they could. When they were done, she handed him the pieces of her shirt and the part of his that he'd used to stanch the bleeding.

They'd been walking parallel to the river, but upstream. Logan just hadn't known where else to go.

So Maddie took the bloodiest of the rags and wrapped them around a rock, tying them over and over. She walked to the tree line and pulled back her arm to throw, but she winced and almost went to her knees. She would have if Logan hadn't caught her.

"I've got you," he said. She looked back at him, over her good shoulder. He could have sworn she let him take a little more of her weight, leaned into him with a little more softness.

He snaked his hand down her arm, then took the bundle from her hands.

"Let me."

He pulled back his strong right arm and threw as hard as he could.

In the center of the river, where the current was strongest, the water hadn't iced over. That was where the bundle landed. Logan knew it without seeing it, without hearing the telltale plop.

The bundle was gone. The rags were at the bottom of the river. But Maddie was still in his arms and she was still shaking.

They'd cut away the blood-covered portion of her clothing, and he helped her pull everything else back on. When he tried to zip her into his coat again, she shook her head.

"You need it," she said.

"You're in shock, Mad. You have to get warm." He tried again to wrap the coat around her, but Maddie was gaining her stubbornness even if not her strength.

"You're bigger than I am."

"Exactly." He shook the coat out again and reached for her.

"Which means if you go down, we're both in trouble. I need you, Logan." The words hurt her. But she said them anyway because there were too many things in those woods that could hurt them. Maddie wasn't the kind of girl who was willing to be killed by a secret. "I need you to be OK."

Slowly, Logan nodded. He pulled on his coat and zipped it up, placed the hood over his head.

"Now what?" he asked her.

She was finally bundled inside her own clothes and standing on her own feet, but they were both running on fumes.

"We walk," she said, then gave one last look across the river, to the place where some unknown man hunted them for some unknown reason. "We try to get as far away from here as possible."

Chapter 19

Dear Logan,

Did you know grizzly bears are always brown and black bears aren't always black, but black bears are never grizzlies?

I know a lot more than that, you know. But I'm not going to tell you because you never answer my letters.

Maddie

Maddie wasn't as cold as she should have been, and that was just one of the things that scared her.

The first sign of hypothermia was the shaking. The second was when the shaking stopped. Her first winter, her dad had sat her down and gone through it all. How important it was to stay warm. How staying warm didn't matter if you couldn't stay dry. She knew the most dangerous thing about the cold wasn't what it did to your body; it was what it did to your mind.

There were lots of cases of people getting so cold that

they thought they were warm. They'd pull off their coats and shoes. They'd run out into the snow and the ice. Hypothermia made you stupid, and in Alaska, stupid would almost always get you killed.

That was why Maddie tried to pretend she was steadier on her feet than she was – why she kept talking, praying that her words wouldn't slur.

They had to keep walking. Keep moving. Because the rule of the wild is simple, and the order is not up for debate.

Shelter before fire.

Fire before water.

Water before food.

Food before pretty much anything else.

So step one was shelter. And the trees no longer counted.

"Keep an eye out for caves," she told Logan. "And sometimes you can crawl into the big trees, nest in around the roots. But we have to be careful."

"Because of bears?" Logan asked.

"And wolves," she said. "Wolves like places like that."

"Oh. There are wolves now. Yay," Logan said.

"If we find a big rock or something with shelter on one side, we can cut some brush and make a lean-to. We need cover. We have to get dry."

It felt like she was talking to herself – like when she was a little girl and she didn't want to go to sleep. She was always stubborn, her father told her. She'd chatter away for hours, and the heavier her eyelids got the louder she talked. She was doing it again, she knew, but this time she didn't care.

"Which way is the bridge?" Logan's voice was filled with concern as he stopped and surveyed their surroundings.

It was pitch-dark, of course. But a little moonlight filtered through the trees, and in a way the snow was a good thing. It covered their tracks and reflected what light there was, and their eyes had adjusted to the darkness. They could walk a little farther. But Logan didn't sound so sure.

"I'm turned around." He sounded panicked. He cursed. "Mad, I'm turned around."

"North is this way," she said. "The river's behind us, but it bends. We're OK."

"But where's the good bridge?"

"Behind us," she said. "He won't catch us. Not yet."

Maddie knew what Logan was thinking – fearing. She knew because she was thinking it, too. She stopped and looked up at him.

Which was a mistake.

Because he was even more handsome than he had been when he'd climbed out of the helicopter, all clean and styled and official.

Now it looked like he needed to shave, which was more than a little scary because

(A) *Logan shaved!*

And (B) it turned out, when pretty tall, pretty handsome boys needed to shave they became less "pretty" and more … handsome. Which was its own particular brand of terrifying.

His eyes seemed brighter in the darkness, his senses more alive. She tried not to remember how warm and safe she'd felt in his arms, but she kept looking up at him, trying to see her friend there. But her friend – her Logan – really was gone. And this boy – this almost-a-man – wasn't nearly as easy to hate as Maddie had been pretending.

Maybe that was why the trees started to swirl, why the sky began to spin.

She just knew that a moment later Logan's arms were around her again, and he was saying, "Whoa there."

"I'm not a horse," Maddie managed to mutter, but her heart wasn't in it. Even she could hear the words slur.

"Yeah. True. So maybe I need to give you a ride."

She wasn't exactly sure what that meant. After all, slang was constantly changing and Maddie had missed six whole years of teenage evolution. In Maddie's world, it was basically 1890, and that wasn't going to change anytime soon. So she had no idea what Logan was saying, but then her feet were off the ground and she was back in Logan's arms and he was walking.

"Put me down!" She hit him on the shoulder, but the blow just glanced off. Because he was so big. Or because she was so weak. Or both.

It was probably both, Maddie realized with something resembling indignation.

She was going to be really mad at herself as soon as she woke up. But that was later. Right now, sleep sounded so much better than fighting.

Sleep sounded like the most brilliant idea in the history of the world.

It had started snowing again – harder now – and Maddie let herself turn her face into the expanse of Logan's broad chest, burrow into his warmth.

She didn't want to close her eyes, but her eyelids had a different opinion on the subject.

She was floating again, drifting. Her shoulder didn't hurt. Her stomach didn't growl. But the forest kept swirling, faster and faster, and Maddie was perfectly willing to go swirling down the drain with the rest of the world.

But then she felt something jerk. Bounce. She started awake.

"Stay with me, Mad Dog."

Logan was there – that was right. It wasn't a dream. Was it?

Maybe it was.

"Maddie, stay with me!" he said again, and Maddie remembered she was in his arms and they were walking.

No. Logan was carrying her.

Logan, whom she hated. But then she thought about the bridge, the look in his eyes when he'd asked *What letters?* and Maddie's hate faded. It got covered by the blowing snow.

"Logan?"

"Yeah?'

"You're gonna wear yourself out," she told him.

"No, I'm not. And you're going into shock, Mad."

Maddie changed her mind again. The new worst part about their situation was that he was right. And he knew it.

"The bullet went straight through. I'm—"

"Stubborn," he finished for her. "When was the last time you ate anything?"

"There were the berries," she told him.

"That's what I thought," he said, and Maddie knew he didn't have a whole lot of room to talk. It's not like he and Stefan had hit a drive-through on their trek through the forest.

Maddie wanted to argue. But she decided to argue with her eyes closed.

There really was something inherently peaceful about being carried. No wonder babies seemed to like it.

"No. Not that easy," Logan said, and shook her again, like he wanted to toss her up in the air and catch her but he changed his mind at the last minute – just a jarring little bounce where she never even had to leave his arms. "Keep talking to me, Mad Dog. How else are the should-be-hibernating-by-now bears going to know to get out of our way?"

The stupid idiot boy with the sexy stubble had a point.

She turned her head to look up at him. He didn't even seem winded even though Maddie knew that she was heavy – she worked so hard and had so much muscle that she couldn't possibly be light.

"Logan?"

He glanced down at her. "Yeah, Mad Dog?"

"What did you mean? When you said that your dad hates you."

He walked on for a little while. There was nothing but the sound of his new boots crunching in the snow and the ice, the breaking of twigs and the wind in the trees. For a moment, she wasn't sure if she'd actually said the words aloud or not. Maybe she hadn't. Maybe this was the dream.

"Logan?" she said again, her voice softer than it should have been.

"I meant that the president hates me," Logan said at last, but it didn't make any sense. *Nothing* about anything made sense anymore to Maddie, not the least of which was why Logan was talking about his father like the man was a stranger.

"No, Logan. I know your dad, remember? He—"

"You don't know my dad, Mad Dog." Logan sounded like a man who wasn't in the mood to fight anymore.

Logan sounded like a man.

"But ..." Maddie wanted to argue, but she didn't remember how. She just knew that sleep was the most wonderful thing in the world and the boy who was carrying her wouldn't let her do it.

"You know who he was when he was hanging around with your dad. You know who he is when the cameras are rolling. When the cameras aren't rolling ..."

Maddie knew what he was saying then, even though the words didn't make any sense. Even though they might very well have been a part of this very cold, wet and utterly surreal dream. She was going to wake up any moment and curse herself for letting the fire go out.

But the hurt in Logan's voice ... She shifted and looked up. The pain in Logan's eyes was real.

"I'm smarter than he is. Did you know that? They had me tested. And my scores were ... They were really high."

"You sound like that's a bad thing."

"Do you know what he said? When they got my scores? He said 'Now you don't have any excuses.'"

"Excuses for what?"

Logan shivered in a way that had nothing to do with the cold. "Imperfection. They had quantifiable proof that I could be perfect if I just wanted to be."

"Logan—"

"So I stopped wanting to be." He looked down at her, fat white snowflakes clinging to his dark lashes. "But there was one time I wish I had been."

"What does that mean?"

"It means that if I'd been just a little smarter, I could

have stopped them before your dad got hurt. And if your dad hadn't gotten hurt, then maybe …"

He couldn't say the words, so Maddie said them for him. "Then maybe I wouldn't have left."

Logan walked faster then, with new purpose. As if the wolves were on their heels.

"It's not your fault, Logan. If it hadn't been for you, your mom would have been taken. She probably would have died. You're the one who saw her dress. You're the one who remembered to press your panic button and get help. You saved her."

He looked down at her. "I lost you."

Maddie didn't know what to say to that. He wasn't walking anymore. He was just standing in the snow and the cloudy streaks of moonlight, staring down into her eyes like maybe it wasn't too late to go back, do it all again.

But there were no second chances. Life didn't work that way, and Logan, genius that he was, was smart enough to know it. So he looked back to the trees and kept walking.

"I don't know why, you know?" Maddie's voice was faint, but she ran a hand across Logan's chest, like she was trying to feel his heartbeat through his coat. "One day he was in the hospital and the next he was coming home. But he wasn't home. Not really. He just told me to pack a bag and the next thing I knew we were here and we had other lives."

"Your dad loves you, Mad Dog."

There was awe in his voice. And envy.

Maddie hated every word.

"Logan, no. You're wrong. Your dad loves you, too."

Logan laughed then, and it was colder than the wind.

He started walking faster, away from the man who was chasing them, away from the risk that, in a way, had been on his trail for six long years and might never, ever stop.

"Rest, Mad," he told her.

"I thought I was supposed to keep talking."

"Yeah." Logan laughed a little. "I forgot who I was talking to."

"We're going to be OK."

Maddie was an excellent liar. When you talked as much as she did, you get good at saying all kinds of words. She could even convince herself most of the time. She'd gotten especially good at that in the past six years.

It's not that cold in here.

Elk meat is delicious and tastes like chicken.

It's almost impossible to get sick of salmon.

(Even though it is very, very possible to get sick of salmon.)

But the biggest lie was this: *I don't even need people anymore.*

Maddie needed her father. And Maddie needed Logan, even when he was just a memory or a name on a letter. Even when he was just someone to hate. Long before he was the boy who bound her wounds and kept her warm and carried her through the forest, she needed him.

Her darkest, deepest fear was that a part of her always would.

"You're not shaking anymore," Logan told her, looking down.

With the snow still falling and the ice in the trees, it was almost beautiful. It was almost like a dream. The good kind, for once.

"Mad?" He couldn't hide the worry in his voice or in his eyes. "You're not shaking anymore!"

"I feel fine," she told him.

"No. You don't feel anything. That's worse."

"It feels better," she said, even though she knew that he was right.

"We need to get you to a hospital."

"There is no hospital, Logan. There's no help."

"Then what is there?" he snapped. He didn't mean to. Maddie could see the remorse in his eyes as soon as he said it. He opened his mouth, as if to apologize, but then it felt like a movie again.

The snow stopped falling.

The clouds actually parted.

The moon sliced through the darkness, like a spotlight through the trees.

And there it was.

It was covered in ice, and snow had blown up against it, a drift that might have hidden its silhouette. But Maddie knew the shape of a roof when she saw one. Maddie knew miracles when she found them.

"There's that," she said, and Logan followed her gaze to the tiny cabin that sat a little higher on the hill.

Chapter 20

Dear Logan,

I really miss you. And I'm mad at you. But not as mad as I am at myself for continuing to write you these letters.

Maddie

It wasn't more than a shack, but the sight of it must have been enough to stun Logan, because he didn't complain when Maddie slid from his arms.

Then stumbled.

Her head spun a little, and she felt his arms around her again, but he didn't lift her. He just held her as they tried to climb the rise of the hill towards something that wasn't quite a cabin, wasn't quite a shack. But it was there. And it had a roof and walls and there was a stovepipe sticking out of the snow on top of the slanting roof.

"What is that?" Logan asked, and Maddie could see where he'd be confused.

"It's a trapper's shed," she said, then stopped. Every

one of her senses seemed to go into overdrive as she looked around at the glowing white stillness, as she listened to the wind. Branches cracked under the weight of the snow and the ice, but not even the birds were moving out there.

They were alone.

For now.

"Logan, did you bring us here because you saw it on Stefan's map?"

The map and the bridge and the man seemed a million miles away. It seemed like it had happened last year. Six years ago. It was another lifetime. Everything had changed since waking up in Logan's arms.

Logan must have felt it, too, because he shook his head as if trying to shake off some foggy dream. "I … No."

"Think, Logan. If it was on the map, then he'll know it's here. We can't stay here." She looked at the snow-covered ground. Their footsteps stood out like neon in the moonlight. Now that Maddie was upright again – thinking again – she wanted to panic.

She looked up at the sky and prayed that the clouds would come back, that the snow would fall harder and cover their tracks.

It had been falling steadily for at least an hour. Maybe if they were lucky their steps near the bridge would be covered by the time Stefan made it there.

But Maddie felt like she hadn't been lucky in a very long time.

"Logan, think!" she snapped. "Was it on the map?"

Maddie knew him. Not the president's kid. Not the tabloid troublemaker. Maddie knew the boy who had been so freakishly smart and helplessly awkward that he had been willing to befriend the girl who never shut up. Just so he wouldn't have to do any talking.

Maddie knew Logan's secret. She didn't need to give him special tests to know the truth. Logan had seen that map. Which meant Logan would *remember* that map. He had to.

"Logan," she whispered. "Look."

So he closed his eyes. He shook his head. "It wasn't on there."

And Maddie felt herself sway again, falling into his arms.

Logan didn't want to cry. It wouldn't be manly, for starters. And for some reason, since seeing Maddie again, he felt the need to be as manly as possible. He didn't let himself think about why.

But mostly, Logan didn't want his tears to freeze. It would be the only part of him that wasn't frozen.

Like a guy who swears he isn't hungry until he actually smells food, Logan didn't know how cold he'd been. He didn't realize how hard it was to keep moving one foot in front of the other until he was moving towards a roof and four walls.

Going was one thing. But to go on and on, walking indefinitely towards nothing, was much worse.

It wasn't because he carried Maddie. No, just the opposite, in fact. Maddie's weight in his arms was what had kept him moving forward, what gave him his strength. Logan had no idea where they were going, but he knew what he was doing – he was getting Maddie to safety. It was the only thing worth doing. And he was going to do it if it killed him.

But now that the shack was in sight, Logan's legs wanted to falter. He wouldn't let them, though. Not now that Maddie was as white as the snow and teetering, unsteady as they climbed the hill.

Snow had drifted in front of the door, but there was no lock, and when Logan pushed against the wood it opened into the small, dark space that was just as frigid as the air outside. The drift collapsed, snow falling over the threshold and dusting the floor, but at least they were out of the wind here. They were at least a little safe from whatever predators might be filling the woods.

Or *some* of the predators, at least.

Logan hadn't lied to Maddie. The shack wasn't on Stefan's map. But he also knew that he'd left footprints. A day's worth of sleet had turned the ground to ice, and the snow was a fluffy blanket atop it. More had fallen, and the wind was blowing, but they could be tracked. It was possible. But there was nothing he could do about it, and he didn't dare mention his fears to Maddie, even though he knew she must be thinking the same thing. There are some worries that are just better if they're never said aloud.

"Oh, thank goodness." Maddie nearly doubled over in relief when she saw the small black cast-iron stove.

There was a matchbox sitting atop it and Logan bolted for it. "Empty," he said, tipping the box upside down to prove his point. Disappointment roiled within him, and he threw the empty box at the wall.

"We don't need it," Mad told him.

"But—"

"Not when we've got that."

He turned and saw the corner of the shack where wood was stacked and dry and waiting.

"Somebody up there loves us," Logan said. He actually bent down and kissed a log. It tasted like safety.

Maddie laughed at him, and that was the best thing in the shack, Logan decided. The sound of Maddie's laughter.

"That's a rule here," she told him. "There are cabins like this scattered all over, built by hunters or trappers or whatever. But if you use the wood, you replace it." She got a little somber. "You could be saving someone's life."

Then Logan remembered the matches. "Lot of good it does us without matches."

Maddie sounded insulted. "Bring me the box."

"Mad Dog, it's empty," he reminded her. Maybe the hypothermia was getting worse. Maybe she was starting to not think straight.

But she sounded just like Maddie – just like Old Maddie – when she said, "Will you bring me the box, *please*?"

So Logan did as she asked.

She eased open the door of the little stove. It was dusty and the hinges squeaked, but everything seemed OK. At least it did in the dark.

Logan watched as Maddie tried to tear at the cardboard of the box, but her hands shook. She was weaker than she'd ever admit, so he placed his hand over hers, took the box, and ripped.

"How small do you want the pieces?"

"Tear it into strips and make a little nest in the stove. Then go strip the bark off some of those birch logs."

"OK," Logan said.

She was unzipping her coat, but it wasn't the hypothermia playing tricks on her, Logan was sure. He watched as she pulled on the chain that was around her neck, tugging something out from beneath her many layers.

The breath she drew was deep and shaky and almost reverent as she looked down at the small items in her hands.

"I was terrified he was going to take them," she said, but Logan couldn't imagine why. They were the most un-Maddie-like pieces of jewelry he had ever seen, but she held them like they were precious.

Like they were life itself.

"Here," he told her when he came back with the pieces of bark. "Is this enough?"

"Yes," she said, and took the biggest piece.

Logan knew a lot of things, not the least of which was when to get out of the way. That was the first thing he'd learned as a toddler in the governor's mansion. So he sat down and scooted back and watched Maddie make a small nest of the cardboard pieces inside the stove. Then she reached into her pocket and pulled out her little tube of Vaseline, but her hands were too cold and she could barely work the lid.

"Uh, Mad Dog, maybe your lips can wait?"

"You're more than welcome to wait outside," she said as she spread some on her lips. She smirked, then started spreading Vaseline all over one of the pieces of cardboard and wadding it up. By the time she placed it on the biggest piece of bark it was a tiny, greasy ball.

Her hands shook as she worked. She was so pale. He had to get her warm, but he knew better than to rush her.

"This is a firesteel," she explained, taking the necklace off and holding up a small metal rod. Then she held up the other piece. "And this is magnesium."

It wasn't big, maybe the size of a pack of gum. And Logan watched as Maddie carefully ran her knife along the magnesium block, shaving off little pieces that fell onto her oily piece of cardboard.

"Magnesium shavings are really flammable, and they burn super hot."

"Yeah. Four thousand degrees," Logan filled in.

"That's right." Maddie sounded shocked. And

disappointed. Like maybe she couldn't call him an idiot anymore.

"That's why this works even when it's wet. It's better than matches," she explained.

"What about the Vaseline?"

"It's oil. The cardboard is a candle now, basically. Usually, you need the Vaseline. Or you need the magnesium. But tonight ..."

"We need both?" Logan guessed.

She looked up at him. "I'm not taking any chances."

"What can I do?" he asked. He was feeling restless, desperate.

"Pray." She held the little rodlike piece of metal close to the ball, then brought the dull side of her knife to it and waited a moment, drew a deep breath before swiping her knife down the little rod.

Sparks flew, lighting the air. For one brief moment that frozen shack was full of fireflies. For one split second it was summer.

But then, just that quickly, it was gone and darkness filled the cabin. Logan could hear Maddie's breath rattle. Even in the shadows, he could see her hands shake.

Maddie didn't seem deterred, though. She acted like this happened all the time, being stranded in a blizzard a hundred miles from a hospital with nothing but a tiny, flickering spark standing between you and certain death.

Logan refused to think about the certain death part, so instead he looked at the girl.

A little blood was still in her hair; he could see it when the sparks flew again. He thought about the Maddie he used to know. She would have never been seen with her hair like that, with her face dirty and her nails broken. But that girl hadn't been silly. She hadn't been vain. She was just … bedazzled. And she was still before him, certain and strong and saving his life.

"You can do it," he reminded her. "You're Maddie Freaking Manchester. You used a bear trap on a really ticked-off Russian. You can start a fire."

So Maddie pulled her knife down the rod again. Sparks flew from the end and, in a flash, one of them caught.

Logan actually held his breath as Maddie blew on the tender flame, then transferred the little burning ball to the nest of cardboard inside the stove and surrounded it with more of the bark, careful not to smother the flames that were growing stronger and brighter and hotter with every moment.

As Maddie started adding bigger pieces of wood to the fire, Logan looked at her in the light. She still looked like his Maddie, but she was so much more now.

"It's a shame we didn't have any nail polish remover, huh?" he teased. He needed to hear her laugh again. Everything was OK when Maddie laughed.

But Maddie *didn't* laugh.

Instead, her head jerked up, almost like she'd heard a shot, seen a bear. Logan actually jolted, looking around. But Maddie was staring right at him.

"What did you just say?"

"I said it's a shame we don't have any nail polish remover. But I guess lip stuff will do." He looked down at the small flame that was slowly coming to life. An orangish glow washed over Maddie's face and she was maybe the most beautiful thing he'd ever seen. Or she would have been. If she hadn't looked like her best friend had just died. Again.

"Why did you say that?"

Logan wanted to laugh, tell her she was talking crazy, being so much of a girl.

"Why did you say that, Logan?" she practically shouted.

And Logan remembered the truth. The lie.

She'd been so mad, so … hurt. He hadn't thought … But that was the problem, wasn't it? Logan didn't think anymore.

"Logan, why—"

"I told you, Mad Dog," he said at last. He made himself meet her gaze. "I remember everything I read."

Chapter 21

Logan was thawing. Maybe it was the fire that was growing, throwing light around the cabin and putting off the sweetest heat that he had ever felt. But more likely it was the rage that was coming off of Maddie, burning like the sun.

She pushed herself across the cabin floor. Dust mixed with melting snow, and she didn't even care that they had come there to get dry. At that moment, she just had to get away from Logan.

"You read my letters? You got them. And you read them. And you never wrote me." The cold came again. "*You lied.*"

"Maddie—"

"You … Why didn't you write me, Logan? Why?"

"Because you were gone!" Logan didn't know where the words came from or why he was shouting. He just knew that a hurt he thought was gone was pouring out of him and he couldn't stop it. Everything was too raw, too primitive. "You left. And you were better off."

"Do you think I *wanted* to go?" Maddie asked him. "If you really read my letters, you would have known ... You would have known how it was." Her voice broke, and Logan knew how much that simple fact must have hurt her.

He pushed his hood back, ran a hand through his hair. "I didn't write to you, Mad, because I wanted you to stop writing to me."

"But why?" Maddie sounded like someone who had been waiting her entire life to ask that question. She looked like someone who would wait a lifetime more for an answer.

"Because you weren't just my best friend. You were my *only* friend. And I almost got you killed." He laughed a little, cold and dry. "Looks like that's a bad habit."

"I don't believe you," she told him.

"Fine. Don't believe me. But I know from personal experience that when your only friend leaves, sometimes the best thing you can do is try to convince yourself she never existed."

Logan hadn't thought that Maddie could go any paler, but she did. She swayed a little again, and he remembered her head and her shoulder. She was so small. She'd lost so much blood.

"I'm sorry if my letters were such a burden to you. I'm sorry I was anything to you."

Logan would have rather faced Stefan, the snow, a

bear – anything but the look in Maddie's eyes before she turned from him. The bullet looked easy in comparison to the pain that he had caused. When she reached for a pan that had overturned and was lying on the dusty floor, she winced, and he bolted towards her.

"Let me," he said, but she climbed to her feet without help.

"We need snow," she said, and Logan knew she wasn't asking for help so much as she wanted to be alone.

"I'll do it," he said, then he took the pot and went outside. She needed a minute. He needed a minute. Those were the lies he told himself, but the truth was they both needed the past six years back. Only six years would do.

Logan filled the pot with snow, then pushed it around and dumped it out a few times to try to clean the dust away. Then he filled it with the cleanest, freshest-looking snow he could find, brought it back inside, and set it on the stove.

Maddie didn't face him.

Her coat and shirt were off and drying by the fire. She stood in her tank top, twisted at a strange angle, wincing.

"Maddie?"

"I'm fine," she snapped.

"You're not fine," he told her, and forced her to turn around. She'd found an old first aid kit and a bottle of booze and was trying to pour it on her wound, but the angle made it hard.

"Let me," he said, taking the bottle from her and pulling away the pieces of fabric they'd tried to use to stop the bleeding. He tossed the bloodiest of them in the fire, but when he opened the bottle and held it over the wound, he hesitated.

"This is going to hurt," he said.

And the look in her eyes almost killed him. "I've been hurt before."

When the alcohol hit the bullet wound, Maddie didn't even wince. She didn't say a word as he bandaged her up and put more wood on the fire. This was the same girl who'd once talked nonstop throughout the entire flight from DC to London, but now she acted like she'd never speak again.

"Maddie …"

She was moving then. There were some blankets on a shelf and Logan sighed with pleasure. When she found a pair of sweatpants and a flannel robe he almost wept with joy. But when Maddie started to undress, he panicked.

"What are you doing?"

"We've been in the freezing rain and snow all day, Logan. The fire isn't going to do us any good if we're both wet through. We'll chill. We will never get warm if we don't get dry, and we won't get dry if we don't …" She trailed off but gestured at her body. It was OK. Logan knew exactly what she was saying.

"Turn around," she told him.

"Mad, I don't know …"

"If you want to die, keep your clothes on. If you want to live long enough to get out of this mess, then turn around and strip. Put those on." She tossed him the sweatpants and a blanket. They were musty and cold, but they were also dry, unlike every layer of his clothing.

He risked a glance over his shoulder and saw a pale arm disappear into the robe.

He could hear Maddie moving a little, saw her laying out her clothes near the fire. Steam actually rose from her jeans and she leaned down to put another log in the stove. It was still far from hot in the cabin, but he wasn't shaking anymore and neither was she.

So he did as he was told, stripping off his wet things and then slipping into the sweatpants and wrapping the blanket around his shoulders.

"Come here," she told him.

The snow in the pan was melted, and Maddie found something like a cup and dipped it in, brought the warm water to Logan's lips.

"Tasty," he said.

Then he took the cup and got some water, held it out for her and she sipped. It felt like some kind of ritual. Like maybe now nothing could tear them asunder.

"We're not going to die here," Maddie told him. Logan held his hand over hers around the cup and took another sip.

He couldn't look away from her. "Of course not. That would be a terrible way to die. Your hair would be stuck like that. Probably forever."

She hit him on the shoulder, but she was smiling, and everything inside of Logan began to thaw.

He took another sip of water, then offered one to her. The water was starting to warm him from the inside, but Logan's stomach was still empty. It growled, the sound filling the little shack. Outside, the wind howled. There was a tiny window with grimy glass, and Logan could see that the snow had started to fall again.

"That's good," Maddie said, following his gaze. "It should cover our tracks and hide the smoke from the fire. We should be safe here."

Maddie looked around the tiny shack again, four walls barely thicker than cardboard, a hard wooden floor, raised a foot off of the frozen ground. But there was that black stove and a large stack of wood and a pot full of warm water, and that was enough to save their lives.

When she looked back at him, something in Logan broke in two because Maddie – his Maddie – was there, in that glance. Her full bottom lip started to tremble in a way that he knew had absolutely nothing to do with the cold.

"We're gonna—"

"Hey—"

They both spoke at exactly the same time. Logan smiled at her. "After you."

Maddie sank down to the hard floor, to the place where the fire was the hottest, right in front of the stove's open door. The wood was turning red and sparks flew occasionally, but Maddie didn't scoot away. She just wrapped her arms around her legs and brought an extra blanket around her like a cape. She looked like a superhero: Survival Girl. Logan had no doubt she'd save the day. In fact, she already had.

He sank down beside her. His raincoat wasn't far away, and Logan could tell that it was already dry, so he pulled it close and draped it around both of their shoulders as they huddled closer to the fire.

There was nothing but the howling of the wind and the cracking and popping of the burning wood. And six long years of unanswered letters and even more unanswered questions.

"Mad—" Logan started just as Maddie said, "Remember those little cheese biscuits the White House chef used to make?"

Logan forgot what he was going to say. He laughed instead. "Remember them? I had one two days ago."

She turned to look up at him. "I miss those."

He looked down into her huge eyes. He pushed a curl away from her face. "I missed those, too. I missed them more than I can ever say."

And they both knew that they weren't talking about biscuits anymore.

When Logan put an arm around her, she didn't pull away. This time, she leaned into him. Maybe for warmth, but Logan didn't think so. He tried to wrap the jacket tighter around her, but then he bolted upright and moved away.

"I almost forgot."

He reached into the jacket pocket and pulled out a bunch of berries, held them towards Maddie like an offering. "Are these the good kind?"

"Yes!" Maddie said, then launched towards them. She put one in her mouth and chewed, then smiled. "These are a kind of cranberry, but be careful. There's a poisonous berry that looks a lot like them. So if we find more tomorrow, check with me before you eat anything, OK?"

"OK," Logan said. He wanted to smile, watching Maddie talk. It was almost like old times.

"I'll catch something to cook in the morning. I don't think we're far from the river. There will be fish."

"You can do that?" Logan eyed her. Maddie eyed him back, a little offended.

"I caught a Russian killer."

Logan ate another berry. "Point taken."

They ate in silence for a while. When Maddie stopped to lick the juice from her fingers, Logan couldn't help himself.

He blurted, "I thought you were dead."

Maddie stopped eating and looked up at him. "I'm not."

She put a finger in her mouth again, and Logan told her, "Don't do that."

"Do what?" she asked, almost with a shrug.

"Don't die on me again. Ever."

Her hair was drying quickly in the heat of the fire, and it was turning into curls. He tugged one of the rings gently.

"OK," she told him.

"And don't come back for me again. No matter what happens. I want you to run. To save yourself. Don't do something stupid just to get me a key. Even if your key delivery system was … unexpected."

"You don't mean that, Logan."

He laughed. "Oh, I wasn't expecting it. I promise."

"No." She pushed his hand away. "I mean … I'd do it again."

"So would I," Logan said, and then he couldn't help himself. He was leaning closer, drawn towards her like a magnet. Maddie was his true north, and he couldn't turn away from her then, not if his life depended on it.

Even if hers did.

He was growing closer and closer and then her lips were on his again, warmer now. She tasted like snow and berries and it was the sweetest thing that Logan had ever known.

When he pulled away he kissed her again on her forehead. Her blanket had fallen and the robe gaped a little, so he placed a quick kiss on the stretch of skin between her neck and the strap of her tank top – not far from the place where she'd been shot.

Maddie was shot, Logan reminded himself, then pulled away. But when she lay down before the fire, Logan could do nothing but spoon himself behind her, pull as many of the warm blankets around them as possible.

She put her head on his chest, and he put his arm around her shoulders and it was the single best moment of Logan's life.

Only one thought was able to ruin it.

"Mad, what happens tomorrow?" he asked.

The fire cracked again, and sparks flew.

"Tomorrow we make a phone call."

Chapter 22

For the third time in two days, Maddie woke up feeling like she was lost inside a dream.

She was too cold, but also too hot. An unfamiliar weight was draped across her waist, and she really, really needed to fluff her pillow. But then Maddie's eyes flew open, and she saw a stove that was full of hot coals and not much else. She shivered and realized that she was wearing her base layers and a threadbare robe and lying on a scratchy blanket. There was another blanket and some coats on top of her. But the most disturbing things were the arms. Two of them. One was beneath her head and one was wrapped around her waist, heavy and sure. And her hand was holding its hand and something inside of Maddie swore to never, ever let it go.

It wasn't a dream, Maddie realized. And she couldn't decide whether that should make her terrified or ecstatic.

Then there was a too-deep voice in her ear. "Good morning."

Maddie bolted away like maybe she'd been stung. "Yes. Um. Good morning."

Logan pushed upright. At some point in the night he must have gotten up to check his clothes, because he was wearing dry jeans and socks, a white T-shirt stretching across his broad chest.

Very broad.

Oh, so utterly broad that it didn't look at all like the chest that he'd had when they used to go swimming at the White House.

The sun was up, and light filled the little shack, filtering through holes in the walls and the roof and the small, grimy window. But they'd lived. And as soon as they were out of this mess Maddie was going to come back and fill this place with so much firewood and kindling that it might crumble under the weight of it all.

Then she realized Logan was eyeing her like maybe she looked as awful as she felt.

"What is it?" she blurted.

"I didn't know it was possible for hair to even point in that direction." He reached for her head, but she batted his hand away and he burst out laughing.

Maddie tried to run a hand through her hair, but her curls were too wild and windblown. It was all she could do to tuck it behind her ears.

"Better?" she asked.

"Oh, much," he said with so much sarcasm she hit him again. Just for good measure.

But then they both stopped smiling, stopped laughing, and Maddie realized they were still holding hands. It was like they had frozen that way, dried together in some kind of knot just like her hair.

"Did you sleep OK?" Maddie asked, even though she couldn't remember whether or not she'd asked it already.

"Yes. I slept perfectly."

"Oh. OK. Uh ..." She looked down at the place where she'd spent the night, wrapped up in him. "Your arm didn't fall asleep, did it?"

"No." Logan shook his head. The awkward was palpable. Maddie was practically drowning in it, but Logan seemed as cool as the wind. "My arm is perfect."

Then he pulled the blankets and the coats back over Maddie and went to put more wood on the fire. He froze in the act of putting a log on the coals and asked her, "Is this OK?"

Maddie glanced at the dirty window. "I think so. It looks overcast and it's still spitting sleet. No one's gonna see a little more smoke."

"Good." He tossed the log onto the fire, then hopped on the cold floor, jumping over Maddie's legs to land behind her. He sank down and dragged her back into his arms and wrapped the blankets and coats around them both again. It was like a cocoon. Outside the blankets, the world was cold and scary and awkward. *Seriously*, Maddie thought. A person could spontaneously combust from so much awkward. But inside the blankets the world was warm and safe and she didn't have to think about anything. Not about Russian kidnappers or unanswered letters. Not about the bullet or the fall or the lie that hurt more than anything else.

She wanted to close her eyes and sleep again, but when she moved, her shoulder felt like fire and a fresh wave of nausea ran through her body, and she knew that sleep wouldn't save them. For six years, mornings had started with chores, and Maddie knew that she could lie there in Logan's arms and make believe. Or she could get up and do something about it.

So Maddie got up.

"Logan, do you remember the map?" she asked before even really realizing that she'd been thinking about it. Even though some part of Maddie's brain had never *stopped* thinking about it.

"Yes," he said slowly. It was like he was wise to Maddie's cocoon analogy and he was very much Team Stay Inside Where It's Warm.

"Good," Maddie said.

At some point someone must have tried to make this little shack a home because one wall was covered with peeling, faded wallpaper. Maddie reached for her jeans and pulled them on. They were filthy and stiff but they were dry. She slipped off the robe and pulled on the second of her three shirts, then walked to the wallpaper and ripped. A piece came off in her hands.

There were pieces of old burnt wood around the base

of the stove, and Maddie found one that turned her fingers black and handed it to Logan.

"I want you to draw it – as much of it as you can. I want to see what he sees."

She reached for her boots.

"Where are you going?" He acted almost hurt, like he didn't want to be left behind. Again.

"I'm going to go see what I can catch to eat."

"I'll go with you," Logan said, looking around and starting to pull on more of his own clothes.

"No." When Maddie realized she'd snapped she tried to soften her voice. "It's better if I go alone. I need the map. And we need food and we don't have enough time, so—"

"Mad Dog, it's OK." He nodded towards the door. "Go. Bring home the bacon."

There wasn't any bacon.

But there was a stream filled with fish, and Maddie had braved the cold long enough to pull off her tights and catch some (a feat she *never* could have done in front of Logan).

An hour after she'd left she was warm again and in front of the fire. Logan was sitting beside her and they both looked at the fresh fillets that laid atop the big, flat rocks that Maddie had placed directly on the red-hot coals.

"No offense to the White House culinary team, but that's the best thing I've ever smelled," Logan said.

They would have both been perfectly willing to eat the fish raw and call it sushi, but the smell was doing Maddie almost as much good as the fire. It was warming her from the inside out. Or maybe it was just the way Logan sat closer to her now, their arms touching. Sometimes his hand was on her back. A time or two she caught herself leaning against his chest. When their hands touched neither moved away, and they just stayed like that.

Was that weird?

Or was it more weird to move her hand now for no apparent reason? Maddie knew the protocol for moving the president from the Oval Office to the Situation Room during a national security crisis, but she didn't know exactly how long one could – or should – touch the first son before one was at risk of offending the touch*ee* or embarrassing the touch*er*. Or even really which one she was. She didn't remember touching him, after all. She just kind of was.

She just kind of couldn't stop it.

And, Maddie was starting to realize, neither could he.

"Tell me you forgive me, Maddie. Please. You don't even have to mean it. Just say it. For now."

"Logan … "

"I thought I was doing it for you."

And, with that, Maddie finally found it easy to move away.

"I needed you. I didn't have anyone."

"Which is better than having someone who's just going to get you hurt," Logan said, then looked around the cabin and laughed. "Lot of good that did you."

"Logan?" Maddie said, and slowly he turned to her.

"Tell me you forgive me, Mad Dog. Lie if you have to. I can't go out there thinking you don't know how much I ... How much we ... I need you to know that I'd do anything for you. Even give you up."

"Logan." Maddie looked up and found his eyes. The fire crackled and the snow fell, but all Maddie could ask was, "What did he say? When he was on the phone?"

And just like that the spell was broken. Maddie missed the warmth of his fingers against hers, but she acted like it didn't matter.

She told herself it couldn't possibly matter.

The fish sizzled as Maddie took a long stick and moved the fillets around on the big rocks. She watched as Logan wrapped his hands around his knees.

"He was supposed to meet someone somewhere. Maybe last night? Maybe this morning or sometime today? I'm not sure. I don't think he ever said. It was a plane, I think. He said the boat wouldn't be fast enough. I don't know what he meant by that exactly. Seems to me like a plane would stand out."

Maddie turned on him. For a really smart boy, sometimes Logan could be really stupid.

"There are more people with pilot's licenses in Alaska

than there are people with driver's licenses. No one's gonna notice one more small plane. And besides, the Secret Service will start looking for you today if they haven't already. The Russians are running out of time."

He shook his head and pulled his legs tighter. "You don't know that."

"Yes." Maddie forced herself to her feet. She'd already spent too long sitting, waiting. Leaning against someone who might not be there to catch her next time.

"Logan, you are the president's son. And you've been off the grid for almost twenty-four hours. And there's no reality where that goes unnoticed."

He was moving as she spoke, a subtle, rocking shift that he probably didn't even know he was doing. But when she finished he stopped and looked up at her. "And once they notice?"

Maddie pulled on her gloves and used the sleeve of her coat to pull the rocks from the coals. She sat them on the top of the stove and it was all she could do not to fall on the fish fillets and eat them in one gulp.

"Once they notice, they'll try to reach my dad, who is either back and going crazy or is on his way back and will begin going crazy anytime now."

She reached down and picked up a piece of flaky fish, put it in her mouth, and almost moaned with the taste of it. Logan stood and joined her.

"Then they'll pull up all the satellite footage from around the cabin to make sure no one flew you out. After that, they'll know you're on foot. And they'll start looking. We could start a signal fire – if we can find enough dry wood, which is doubtful. And even if we did, the bad guys would probably get here before the good guys, and we don't want to signal the wrong side."

After a few bites, he asked, "Do we head back for your house?"

Maddie thought about it for a long time before admitting, "I don't know. There are weapons there. And the radio. And maybe one of your agents survived? But Stefan could be expecting us to go there, so ..."

All her life Maddie had heard stories of close calls and bad decisions, lucky breaks that made the difference between life and death. How would history judge this morning? She had to wonder. Would they be the idiots who turned back or the fools who didn't?

Maddie had no idea.

"I think if I were him, that's what I'd expect us to do. But I didn't spend as much time with him as you did."

Logan considered it while he ate another piece of fish and then took a sip of the fresh water that they'd melted on the stove that morning.

"Stefan found us there once," he said at last. Then he considered the tiny cabin. "Do we stay here?"

But there was something else in Logan's voice. Maddie felt it, too, as she glanced to the floor where they'd slept, wrapped up in each other, unaware of the world going totally to pieces all around them.

In the light of day, she could see it for what it was: a shack with peeling wallpaper and a soot-stained ceiling, but there were other things, too: a cracked vase on a shelf, a row of oddly shaped rocks, like some child's treasures.

This place had saved their lives, but life was going to be different outside the safety of its four walls. Maddie didn't want to think too hard about how or why.

"Once the clouds clear, someone's bound to see the smoke." She looked down at the last fish fillet, took a tiny piece, and then pushed the rest towards Logan. "I don't like the idea of ... sitting. We wouldn't freeze to death here. Probably. But we could die here just the same. And I don't want to die waiting."

"Me either."

Logan's voice was sure and steady. He sounded like his dad, Maddie thought, but she didn't say so.

"You've got the map?" she asked. He pushed it towards her.

"I think we're somewhere about here." He pointed to a ridge that wasn't far from the river.

"Closer to here," she said, pointing to a spot nearer to the burned-out bridge.

"It felt like we walked longer last night."

She glanced up at him. "That's because you were walking for two."

"I'd do it again," he told her, but he was too serious. Too close. Maddie had to find a way to push him away without touching him, so she laughed.

"I hope I don't have to hold you to that," she said.

"Mad—"

"Dad didn't want me on this side of the river," she cut him off, pointing to the vast, empty places on the map – the nothingness that surrounded them.

"Why?" Logan asked, and Maddie shrugged.

"There was plenty of trouble on our side. I didn't need to go looking for more. What's this X?" Maddie asked, pointing to where Logan had marked the spot. "Was that on his map? Had he drawn it on there?"

"Yes and yes. Or, at least, someone had drawn it on there. But what he was hoping to find in the middle of a lake, I don't know."

Maddie knew. "That's where he was taking you. If they're flying you out, that's their rendezvous point. Land a small floatplane on that lake and load you up. You'd be in Russian airspace in just a few hours."

"Well, let's try to avoid that if at all possible," Logan teased.

"Good plan." Maddie pointed to the opposite edge of the map and thought about their options. "Canada is that way. We could be there in a couple of days. No one would expect us to walk to Canada."

"You were shot yesterday, Mad. You need a hospital. I'm not dragging you through the forest for two days just to get to Canada where who knows how many more days we'd have to walk to find some help."

"You could do it."

"That's true." Logan nodded, sounding sure. "I could carry you. That could—"

"No! *You* could walk to Canada. Logan, listen – I'll slow you down, but you're the one they want. If I could keep him distracted, then—"

"No! I am not leaving you out here with a madman."

"It was just an idea." Maddie shrugged.

"Well, it was a bad one. I'm never …" He trailed off, but there was something in his gaze. "I'm not leaving you alone."

"I didn't want you to be out there on your own either, you know."

"Good," Logan said, as if he didn't quite realize that they weren't arguing anymore.

For a long moment the cabin was silent except for the cracking of the tree limbs outside, the sparks from the dying fire.

"We're going to have to go back for it."

Neither of them said what *it* was. Neither of them had to.

Logan had almost run onto a burning bridge last night because that pack and the phone inside of it were so precious.

That phone was help. That phone was civilization. That phone was a helicopter and a complete squad of Army Rangers or Navy SEALS or whoever happened to be closest.

That phone was a warm bed and a hot meal and a

shower. Oh have mercy – what Maddie wouldn't have done for a shower.

But that phone was also the second-most-obvious source of help, and if they were thinking about it, then Stefan might be as well.

Logan seemed to read Maddie's mind and her worries. "It's suicide."

But Maddie was shaking her head. Logan's fears were still rattling around in there, and despite her best efforts, some of them were even taking root.

"My dad has a sat phone. He's the one person we know we can trust."

"You're right," Logan told her. "And he's already on his way."

"Probably," Maddie said. "I mean, there's no way he risked flying in last night in all that weather. But when he does get back, he's going to come for us. I left markers, but who knows how many of them made it through the storm. They could be under three inches of ice and a foot of blowing snow by now. Dad might not find them. He may need backup. But if we can call him, he can fly to get us. The river will be frozen in places, and Dad can land there. Dad can land anywhere. He can get us and we can get out of here." Maddie studied him. The fire was cooling down, but neither of them went to get more wood. They wouldn't be there long enough to need it, they both seemed to know.

Then Logan shook his head. "I have to try for it."

And for the first time in her life Maddie didn't argue.

Maddie made Logan turn his red coat inside out so the light blue liner was what showed. They ate the last bites of fish. When Maddie opened the door, the sun was bright overhead, reflecting off the smooth, clear palette of white. It was almost too perfect to disturb, so for a moment they both stood on the threshold of the shack and looked back at the dying fire, the old stove, and the place on the floor where they'd slept.

"I live in the most famous house in the world, but ..." Logan trailed off.

Maddie put her hand in his. "This is my favorite, too," she told him.

He squeezed, and they took a step out into a world that was too white – too clean, too new. There were animal tracks in the snow, but no footsteps. Maddie hated that they'd be leaving their own, but there was nothing they could do about that.

All of her senses were on high alert, but she could smell no other fires, see nothing but trees. There was nothing at all man-made for as far as the eye could see.

It felt to Maddie like they were all alone in the universe.

But they weren't.

And that was the scary part.

Chapter 23

The clouds stayed heavy and the sky stayed dim, but all around them the world shone like it was covered with crystals.

Maddie felt Logan at her back, following closely in her footsteps. Literally. As if maybe Stefan or his friends (if he had any) would be less likely to see one set of footprints than they would be to see two. Or maybe they might think it was someone else – someone on their own. But there were no other people for miles and miles around.

That was something it had taken Maddie a long time to get used to. For the first year or so it always felt like the trees had eyes, like someone was watching, listening. Like there was a whole silent, invisible city living up on the hill with a bird's-eye view of all she said or did.

But only the birds had that, Maddie knew now. And the birds, it seemed, weren't talking.

Then it was as if Maddie had summoned one with her thoughts, because she heard a cry overhead and saw a bald eagle sweeping low, just above the snow-covered canopy of the trees.

"Was that …?" Logan asked.

"We have a lot of eagles here. You can see their nests if you know where to look. They're huge sometimes. Like houses. They mate for life," she said without really realizing what she was saying.

Then she saw Logan's grin and looked back to the path, too quickly.

There was a bush covered with berries nearby, and Maddie pointed at it. "Yummy," she said as she pulled off as many berries as she could, passing a handful to Logan.

They walked a few yards more. Maddie could practically feel Logan's gaze burning into her back. "Yummy," she said, pointing to another bush. She pulled a few more berries and plopped them into her mouth. They were frozen, of course, but the cold, wet juice was a jolt to her system. She had a new bounce, a new purpose to her step when she saw yet another bush.

"Poison," she said, pointing to the third type of berry.

"They look just like all the others," Logan said.

Maddie glanced behind her. "Well, they're not. Trust me."

"So *not yummy*," Logan finished for her.

Maddie couldn't help but smile. "No. Not yummy."

They walked on for a few minutes more, every moment bringing them closer to where they'd started last night, their big head start dwindling with every step.

They moved slower the closer they got. It was like they both knew that any breaking twig or carelessly kicked rock could start an avalanche. Not of snow or of rocks. But of awful.

Yes, Maddie thought with a nod. An avalanche of awful was just one careless step away, so she stepped very carefully indeed.

Logan must have felt it, too, because when he spoke, he whispered. "What are the odds that our friend never found Black Bear Bridge?"

Maddie wasn't surprised at Logan's change of subject. Then again, did it even count as a change of subject if said subject was constantly on one's mind?

In the wintery stillness of the forest it was easy to believe that they were alone, locked together in some enchanted land. But they weren't alone. Eagles flew and tree limbs cracked in the distance, breaking under their icy weight. And forgetting that they weren't the only people in these woods was the most dangerous thing that either of them could do.

Maddie didn't even bother to answer Logan's question. It was an answer they both knew already. So instead she asked, "What would you do? If you were him, what would your play be?"

She could tell by the way he glanced around them that he wasn't going to have to think about his answer. He'd been asking himself that question for hours.

"I'd find Black Bear Bridge and get on this side of the

river, and then I'd find some nice, cozy place to take cover and wait for us. That phone is the best way to get help. It might be the *only* way to get help. And you can bet Stefan knows it."

Maddie nodded. She kept pivoting, looking out across the white horizon just like her father had taught her when she was a little girl and he made his living looking over crowds, scanning for danger. There was never a time in Maddie's life when she didn't know how to scan for danger. Sometimes she wondered what it would be like to *not* know that. Would she have preferred being a normal kind of girl who didn't know what was out there? But, no, Maddie realized. She was the kind of girl who always liked to see things coming.

Logan studied her, read her silence. "It's not too late, you know. We can still walk to Canada. Call it an adventure."

Maddie couldn't help but grin up at him. Logan had always had that effect on her. Spontaneous grinning usually ensued.

"I like Canada," she said. "They have really good donuts."

"They do have good donuts!" Logan exclaimed, as if he couldn't believe he had forgotten that incredibly important fact about one of America's closest allies and neighbors. "And I could learn to play hockey."

Maddie turned. "We could put maple syrup on everything," she said softly.

Then she felt Logan's hand take hers, and she turned

to study him. "We would be really good Canadians."

"Right?"

Logan nodded. "Totally."

But Canada was a world away. They might as well have been talking about setting up camp on the moon.

The wind was colder, but the rain had stopped and they were both dry, for which Maddie was eternally grateful. Still, there was a nagging itch in the back of her mind, a little voice whispering that they weren't out of the woods yet.

They might never be out of the woods.

She looked up at the sky and knew that time was passing. Her father should have landed by now. The alarm should have sounded. Help was on its way, but Maddie had to keep Logan alive long enough for it to get there.

Time was ticking down, Maddie could tell. But towards what, she had no idea.

"How did they find me, Mad Dog?"

"Does it matter now?"

"Yes," Logan practically snapped. "Because there's no use risking our necks to get a sat phone if we have no idea who to call. What if there's a mole in the Secret Service or the White House? What if some secure communications channel got hacked?" Logan took a deep breath. "How are we going to keep from messing up again if we don't know where we messed up to begin with?"

To Maddie, it sounded like an excellent question. But it was one they didn't have time to answer.

"We'll figure that out, Logan. Later. After we call my dad and figure out a place for him to meet us. He can fly us out of here, and then we'll figure it out."

"I don't know." Logan's gaze was trained on the horizon. "Something's wrong." He gestured to the snow and the ice and the thousands of empty acres that surrounded them. "Out there. I can feel it."

Maddie wished she could argue, but she couldn't find the words, so instead she said, "Tell me again, what he said on the phone."

She expected Logan to roll his eyes. The answer hadn't changed in the twenty minutes since she'd last asked.

But Logan was patient as he told her, "My Russian is pretty good, but it's not perfect. And I only heard half of the conversation, but he said that he had to get me somewhere by a certain time – today, I think. I'm not sure what time exactly, but I got the impression that time was of the essence. They were going to be there, waiting and ready."

"Who were *they*?" Maddie asked, but Logan just raised an eyebrow.

"The monster under the bed? The gunman on the grassy knoll?"

"Logan." Maddie wasn't losing patience. But maybe she was losing faith. "Was there a name? A group? An acronym? Anything?"

"A doctor," Logan said. "He said they'd have a doctor there."

"So they don't just want you taken alive," she said. "They're planning on keeping you that way."

"Yeah. Until they aren't."

Maddie could feel it then, the certain knowledge that Logan wasn't as strong as he acted, as cool or as sure as he looked. He was taller. And stronger. And his hands felt better when she held them, and his chest made a much larger pillow than it had when they were ten. She was sure about all that. But Logan was still the same boy he'd been when they were standing in that corridor. He was still terrified he was about to watch someone he cared about get taken away forever. And his deepest fear – the one Maddie could see in his eyes – was that this time, he wouldn't be able to stop it.

"It's going to be OK, Logan. We're going to get the phone and call my dad. He'll tell us where he can land his plane, and then we'll all go to Canada."

"And get donuts," Logan said.

Maddie smiled. "Exactly." She turned and looked out at the frosty wilderness, eyes still scanning, mind still working. "But first we get a plan."

You could hardly tell there'd been a bridge there.

Between the fire and the snow, all the boards were gone, burned or crashed into the water below; the rope had turned to ash. It seemed so much farther down in the light of day, so much so that Maddie wondered if she would have even been able to summon the courage to do what she'd done the night before if she'd been able to see the rocks and the rapids and the ice that lived below.

"It's not that far down." Logan's words were strong, but his voice was significantly less steady.

"Yeah. Totally easy."

"Right?" Logan asked.

"Right," Maddie said.

But neither of them believed it. They stayed hunched behind an outcropping of rocks, higher on the hill. The river curved, and from their hiding place, with a light-colored blanket from the cabin draped over them, they had time to study the deep ravine and look for the pack and the phone and the man they knew had to be out there.

Hunting.

Maddie felt every bit her father's daughter as she scanned the trees and the rocks. She looked up into the icy branches and squinted her eyes, cursing the fact that she didn't have binoculars as she tried to see any footprints in the snow.

"What if he's down there?" she said.

Logan looked at her. "Then I guess we can stop worrying that he'll find us."

It seemed as good a point as any.

Maddie didn't want to wait too long. They didn't want to lose the light, and even with the berries they'd found, that morning's fish was a distant memory. And Maddie's shoulder was starting to burn. The wound needed more than a splash of old vodka and some bandages. She needed a big shot of antibiotics and a bath.

And a hairbrush.

But mostly she needed to get Logan out of there and far away from Stefan and whatever mysterious rendezvous was waiting in the woods.

She cut her eyes up at Logan. "Will it work?"

He grinned back. "There's one way to find out."

The heat that Maddie felt as they eased down the hill, closer to the ravine and the river, had nothing to do with Maddie's wound. It wasn't even the fault of the boy who stayed at her back, glancing over his shoulder periodically, their footsteps light and soft on the slick ground.

When they reached the place where the bridge used to be, Maddie could see that the two posts that had once held the ropes were still standing, but the rest of the bridge was a memory.

She crept closer to the edge and peered over.

"I should go," she said.

"No way," Logan said too loud.

"I've been living here for six years, Logan. I've climbed trees and cliffs and pretty much anything that can collect ice. I can do this. I can—"

Logan didn't argue. He just placed his hand on her shoulder and pressed his thumb against her bullet wound, and Maddie almost passed out from the pain. Stars swirled and her vision went black as she swayed. He hadn't even pressed very hard.

"You were saying?" he asked.

"You don't climb with your shoulder," she tried, but Logan knew better.

"Liar. You climb with your whole body, Mad Dog. And you know it. Even a body as little and adorable as yours."

Two things hit Maddie all at once:

First, the realization that Logan had called her little. And adorable. She wasn't at all sure what that was supposed to mean, but she couldn't possibly stop to figure it out because …

Second, Logan was taking off his coat and pushing up the sleeves of his shirt and she couldn't really stop looking at his forearms. At some point in the past six years Logan's forearms had become the most fascinating thing in the world, and Maddie had no idea how that had happened.

He placed his coat around her shoulders, tugged it tight. "Keep this warm for me, will you?"

Maddie didn't know what to say.

Then Logan was looking over the edge again. Stefan's pack peeked out from beneath the snow one-third of the way down. It wasn't a solid cliff face, but it was close.

"It's not that bad," he said.

"Logan …" She started to argue. A part of her knew she needed to argue, but the part of her brain that was ticking away the moments had stopped sounding like a clock.

It had started sounding like a bomb.

"I'm lighter," she told him.

He looked indignant. "I'm going," he said. And then he grabbed her. And he kissed her. And Maddie thought that maybe Logan's forearms were her second favorite thing.

When he paused and looked over the cliff one more time, he glanced back at her.

"It's a piece of cake," she lied.

But Logan just shook his head. "Man, I miss cake," he said, then eased himself over the edge.

Maddie didn't want to watch Logan's descent. They had discussed this. They knew the risks – Logan knew the risks. They had both accepted them grudgingly, and yet accepting a thing and liking that thing were two incredibly different things indeed.

She watched until he was out of sight and then eased a little way down the edge of the river. She kept an ear tuned to the sound of her father's plane. She kept one eye glued to the sky. Would he set out on foot, looking for them, or would he take the plane and search by air? Maddie couldn't be certain. But she was sure she wasn't alone.

She put the outcropping of rocks to her back.

And waited.

Alone.

Logan would be back soon.

If this plan worked, then they wouldn't have to worry about being chased anymore. They'd get the phone and call her dad and then he'd come get them and fly them far, far away. If this plan worked, then it would soon be over.

Maddie wrapped Logan's coat around her as she stood waiting. Listening.

The forest was full of sounds – rabbits and birds scavenging among the snow. Limbs falling and cracking under the weight of the first ice of the year.

But this was different. A crisp, clean snap.

Maddie spun to her left – looked back to the cliff – but it was too late. He was already there, standing in front of her. The gun was trained on the center of her chest, and the look on Stefan's face was pure, unadulterated loathing.

"You should have forgotten about the phone," he said.

Chapter 24

Maddie had seen evil up close; she'd witnessed terror and rage, and she knew better than most people the effect that pure hate can have on the human body.

First, in Maddie's experience, it was terrible for your skin. (If there was one thing a zit *loved*, it was stress.)

Second, it could do awful things to your eyes. They got glossy, but not with tears, with wild and untamed fury.

Finally, that much adrenaline might make you strong enough to lift a Toyota off a toddler or whatever, but it could also make your hands shake and your heart race.

That's how Stefan looked. His eyes were too wide, his lips were too dry, and his grip was too hard on the gun.

Maddie didn't scream. Or plead. Or cry. She just rolled her eyes and said, "But I'm a teenage girl. We're addicted to our phones, or haven't you heard?"

She could feel the boulder at her back, and as Stefan stepped closer, she knew there was nowhere to go. So she tensed.

"You think you are so smart." Stefan's accent was thicker. The words were cold.

"Well, not to brag, but I am number one in my class. Does it matter if you're the only one in your class?" she asked. "I don't know about—"

"Shut up!" he yelled, limping closer.

Maddie glanced down at the leg that wasn't moving quite right. The bear trap must have gotten him good, she realized. She tried not to smile. He'd wrapped rags around his hands, probably covering up some pretty nasty burns. Maddie thought about the pack that still rested on a ledge one-third of the way down the cliff and wanted to smile because Stefan no longer had his food or his phone or his map.

He didn't even have Logan, and Maddie wondered if he'd been able to make a fire the night before. Honestly, for a second she was simply impressed that he was still alive. He didn't just have a reason to kill, she realized. He had a reason to live. And that fact could prove very useful.

"Your boyfriend should not have left you here."

"He's *not* my boyfriend. I can tell because I don't have his name drawn inside a heart on a single notebook. I swear. And who says he left me? Maybe I left him? Maybe we found someplace safe and I stashed him there."

"I doubt that," Stefan said.

"I'd totally leave him, you know. Boys are annoying."

"True. But there is no safe place. And I am no fool.

I knew you would come for the phone. I have been watching this spot since daybreak. I saw him go over the edge."

Stefan jerked Maddie against him, sliding the barrel of the gun along the smooth skin of her cheek like she needed a shave. "Now you are going to be very still and very quiet, and when he gets back with my phone I promise I will not kill you."

"You're a real sweetie, you know."

"Quiet," he snapped, and placed an arm around her from behind. His big bicep pressed against her neck, but Maddie could look back at him.

"So what's your story?"

Maddie didn't try to hide the singsong lilt of her voice as she spoke. She didn't want to. She'd learned at a very young age that nothing annoyed manly men more than girly girls, and if Maddie had one talent, it was truly exceptional girliness.

"Shut up and be quiet," Stefan snapped.

"That's just a tad redundant, FYI."

"Shut up!" he hissed near her ear.

Maddie couldn't help but shift her weight from foot to foot, almost pacing in place. She was careful of the ice and the snow, though. No use falling to the ground and having Stefan accidentally pull the trigger.

"You really do give a lot of orders," she told him.

He tightened his grip. "I'm the one with the gun."

"Well, yeah. Sure. Technically. But I'm the one

with the winning personality, and that should count for something."

"You should be scared," he said in the same tone a movie villain might use to say *You should be dead* when the hero materializes five years later, hungry for vengeance.

Stefan was confused, and Maddie couldn't blame him.

So she turned back and shrugged. "Maybe. But I don't think you're a bad guy."

He let her go and spun her around, grabbing Logan's unzipped coat and pulling her closer.

"I. Have. The. Gun," he reminded her.

Maddie smiled and pulled away. "And I have Taylor Swift's signature scent. Doesn't make me a pop star. It just makes me smell like Taylor Swift, which isn't as great as it sounds because, to a bear, Taylor Swift smells *delicious*."

Stefan stuttered for a moment, then fell silent. Maddie talked on.

"What makes you think he's gonna care?" she asked. "He's a smart kid. He'll probably see you here, realize you still have the gun, and run for the hills."

Maddie kept her gaze trained on the place where Logan was supposed to be. She only turned when she heard the laughter.

"What's so funny?"

"You are." Stefan actually smiled. It looked so foreign on his gruff face with its two days' growth of beard, his dirty clothes. He looked … handsome. And Maddie was almost entirely certain that she hated him just a little more for it.

"I'm not funny," she snapped. He'd knocked her down a cliff and held a knife to her throat and a gun to her back, but *this* was what Maddie found most offensive.

"Yes. You are. If you think he's not going to move heaven and earth to get you back, you are as crazy as you are stupid. He'll do whatever I say when he sees I have his woman."

For a moment, she couldn't reply. She was breathing too hard, like she'd just had to swim across the lake or climb a cliff or haul a whole elk carcass home by herself.

"If I mean so much to him, I would have gotten a letter at some point in the past six years, but thanks for the optimism. It's been a rough couple of hair days. I appreciate the vote of confidence."

She expected him to grunt something in Russian or threaten her with the gun again. But he just shook his head.

"You do not understand men."

At which point Maddie decided to go ahead and get angry. She jerked away and snapped, "Well, that's just silly, because clearly I've been around *so many of them*!"

She threw her arms out wide and spun, taking in the vast expanse of snow-covered trees and the ice-covered cliffs.

Down below, the river was running faster. The deepest portion hadn't frozen and she could actually hear the roar of one of the waterfalls that cascaded down the face of one of the mountains, a never-ending flow of ice-cold glacier water.

But there were no puffs of smoke, no lights from high school football stadiums or movie theaters or any of the hundreds of things that Maddie imagined must dominate the life of a teenage girl.

There certainly were no teenage boys.

"What?" she snapped when she faced him again. "Why are you smiling?" She wanted to slap that smile off his face for reasons that had nothing to do with kidnapping.

"You remind me of someone," he admitted.

This felt like progress to Maddie, proof that there might actually be a pulse beating beneath that too-broad, too-hard chest.

"Who?" she asked. "Is there a Mrs Evil Assassin back in Mother Russia?"

"No," Stefan said, pulling her back towards him, turning her to make her a human shield. It was like she could actually feel him freeze. "I have no wife. But I do have … a sister."

She opened her mouth to speak, but the gun was pointed at her again, and Stefan was through talking.

But Maddie never quit talking, so she asked, "What's she like?"

"Alive" was Stefan's cold reply.

"She's why you're doing this, isn't she?"

Stefan didn't look scary so much as he just looked scared. And something inside of Maddie actually hurt for him, in that moment. But she also hurt for herself and for Logan, because right then she knew there would be no stopping him. This wasn't about money or politics or even terror. This was personal. And personal was the most dangerous thing of all.

"The president always liked me, you know. You might not even need Logan. I'm enough. Just forget about Logan. You don't need him."

"They do need him," Stefan snapped. "Only him."

Maddie pulled back a little. "*They*, huh? Not *we*?"

Stefan was silent for a moment. Eagles circled overhead, their shadows dark on the snowy ground.

But the darkest part was the look on Stefan's face. "Maybe I will kill you after all."

He raised the gun.

He shook his head.

And a shadow fell across them both as Maddie said, "Now."

In the next moment, a haunting cry filled the air, and Stefan looked around like there must be a wounded bear or some other kind of animal, but there was just a shadow streaking across the sky.

Maddie was barely able to throw herself out of the way

as Logan jumped from atop the outcropping of rocks, hurling himself towards Stefan and knocking him to the ground.

They hit the snow and started to roll, a tangle of limbs and ice and fury. Stefan was older and had some kind of training. But Logan was so terrified and so desperate that he didn't seem to feel the cold or the force of the blows. He didn't even notice how close they'd rolled to the edge of the steep ravine.

He just kept yelling, "Don't touch her! Don't you dare—"

"Logan, stop!" Maddie shouted. The snow was flying as they punched and kicked.

Stefan lashed out, trying to reverse their positions.

They were too close to the edge.

Logan was losing momentum.

So Maddie did the most obvious thing in the world: She ran towards the two of them and kicked Stefan's shin, right where the bear trap must have caught him, because he howled in pain, dropping the gun and bringing both hands to his leg.

And then Logan was on top of Stefan, pressing his head over the edge, like he might just pop it off his neck like the head of a dandelion, let it float away on the wind.

"Logan, stop. Please!" Maddie yelled, but it was like she was far, far away.

Like Logan still had to get her back.

Like he might never get her back.

"Don't you touch her," he growled, looking down at Stefan.

"Logan, stop," Maddie tried again.

But Logan didn't face her. He kept his knees on Stefan's arms and his hands around Stefan's throat. Squeezing.

"He would have killed you."

"Logan."

Stefan's face was turning red and he wasn't making a sound anymore. And Logan seemed to squeeze harder.

Maddie picked up the gun that lay, forgotten, in the snow.

And she fired.

The shot seemed to echo in the cold air, reverberating off the snow and the ice.

Overhead, birds flew away – eagles leaving their nests.

Logan dropped his hold on Stefan, pushed back, and stared up at Maddie.

"What the—"

"Get up." Maddie didn't point the gun at them, but she handled it like someone who would if she had to – like someone who knew how.

"Get up. Both of you," she said. "Before you make me angry."

Stefan actually cut his eyes at Logan. "I'm starting to understand why you didn't reply to those letters."

But it was a bad call because Logan was lunging for him again. "You don't get to talk to her. Or look at her. Or—"

Maddie fired again, the sound filling the air and cutting him off.

Logan jumped to his feet, but Stefan sank lower. He sat in the snow, and all Maddie could think was that his rear was going to get wet. Maddie knew how important a dry rear was to a person's well-being in Alaska, but this probably wasn't the time to say so.

"You might as well kill me," Stefan said.

"OK," Logan said, reaching for the gun.

Maddie jerked it away. "Logan!"

From his place on the ground, Stefan laughed again. "Are you going to kill me, little girl?"

"No," Maddie snapped. "I'm going to tie you to a tree and make you smell like Taylor Swift and then wait for the bears to find you. They'll do it, you know. You'll be praying for a bullet."

Stefan actually shrugged. "OK."

Logan was lunging towards Stefan again, shouting, "Do not tempt me."

Maddie could barely hold him back, but she did. Her arms were around him, squeezing him tight. She tipped up her head and tried to look into his eyes. "Logan, let him tell us why."

"I think we know why," Logan said, but he wasn't fighting Maddie anymore. She kept one arm around him, though. Just in case.

"Logan, look at me. There are at least a half dozen perfectly good reasons why someone would want the president's son." She brought a hand to the stubble on his cheek. "I want to hear what *his* reason is."

When she turned back to Stefan the gun was in her hand, cold from the snow, but solid. She wanted to throw it off the edge of the cliff but knew that would be foolish. Weapons were important in Alaska, even under the best of circumstances. And these were far from ideal.

Stefan had turned his head to look out over the river. The waterfall must have been close, just around the bend, because Maddie could hear it like white noise in her head.

"Well?" Logan prodded.

Stefan turned back to them and looked up, like facing the sun. A shadow crossed his face when he studied Logan. Then he raised his gaze to the sky, to the real sun that was just starting to peak through the heavy clouds.

"Oh, are you running late?" Logan asked. "Please, don't let me stop you if there's someplace you need to be."

"It's too late now," Stefan said. "You win. Is that what you want me to say?"

Maddie shook her head and held Logan back again. "I want you to tell us who they are, Stefan. Do they have your sister? Is it supposed to be some kind of trade? Logan for her?"

But the Russian stayed silent.

"Why?" Maddie asked. "The United States doesn't negotiate with terrorists. Whatever they want Logan for, it won't work."

“This has *nothing* to do with your precious United States.”

For the first time, Stefan’s hands were shaking as he brought them to his face. Maddie had learned six years ago that any kind of animal can be dangerous if it’s hurting or if its young is in danger.

Stefan was both. And even though Maddie had the gun, she was terrified.

“Stefan, she’s OK. Wherever she is, wherever they have her, I’m sure she’s just fine. I’m sure she’s …”

It was the look in Stefan’s eyes that made Maddie trail off, forced her to turn around. She felt Logan turning, too, but he froze just as she lurched towards the man who was bent and bloody and stumbling from the trees.

“Dad?”

Chapter 25

It wasn't Maddie's father. That much was obvious to Logan the moment the man stepped from the shade of the tall trees, out into the bright sunlight that reflected off the snow.

But Maddie wanted her father so badly, she was willing to believe in miracles. And it was a miracle, Logan had to remind himself. Just a different kind.

When Maddie slammed to a stop, Logan knew she must have realized who it really was.

"You. You're not dead," she blurted, even though Logan was pretty sure the forest ranger probably felt more dead than alive at that moment.

Maddie turned her back on Logan and Stefan and ran towards the ranger, who practically collapsed into her arms.

"Heard your shots," he said.

"It's OK. We've got you. You're safe now."

But the ranger's gaze was locked on Stefan. Rage and

pure hatred bloomed on his face, and Logan turned back to the man in the snow and saw a totally different expression: disbelief and also ... fear.

"Step away from him, little girl," Stefan warned.

"No!" Maddie snapped. She pouted. She did everything but stomp her foot, but the gun was still firmly in her grip so no one dared to tell her that she sounded like a child. Probably because she was also a child who was an extremely good shot.

"It's OK. You're OK." Maddie spoke softly to the man. Like maybe he was an injured animal who might not realize she was there to help.

Blood covered his coat and he wasn't terribly steady on his feet, but he was alive and on this side of the river. And when he told Logan, "Step away from that man," his voice was strong and sure.

"It's OK." Maddie held up the gun. "We've disarmed him."

"Good work," the ranger said. "Now get over here," he told Logan, but he never took his gaze away from the man in the snow.

The man who had shot him for no apparent reason.

"Are you OK?" Logan asked, but the ranger shook the question off.

"I should be asking the same of you."

"I'm fine," Logan said. Then he looked at Maddie. "We're fine."

"Good. That makes things easier."

"Makes what easier?" Maddie asked.

Behind Logan, Stefan was yelling in Russian. "*You may be alive. But you will never be a wolf!*"

And just like that Logan was back in that long-ago corridor, listening to the echo of the very first words that Logan had translated from Russian into English: *A boy is no match for a wolf.*

Maybe it was Stefan's words or Logan's memory. Maybe it was the flash in the ranger's eyes, the sign he'd understood the Russian's threat. But more likely it was the tattoo that was peeking out from beneath the ranger's sleeve: a two-headed bird in the clutches of a wolf.

A tattoo that Logan had seen once before.

"Maddie!" Logan and Stefan shouted at the same time, but it was too late. She was too close, her guard too low, and the man pulled her back against him and squeezed her tight, his own gun suddenly pressed to her temple.

Logan's blood ran cold – but Maddie, being Maddie, groaned and said, "*Not again.*"

"You folks need some help?" This time the ranger's words were too cheerful. He sounded borderline insane when he laughed. And when he spoke again, his too-friendly American voice was gone.

This time his accent was cold and hard and Russian.

"I knew you were a coward, Stefan, but you were a fool to try to save this girl as well. Now they'll both die."

Stefan was up, out of the snow and easing forward. "Let her go, Uri."

"Drop it!" the man snapped, squeezing Maddie tighter. "Drop your gun and kick it away." But Maddie just gripped and re-gripped the gun that was still in her hands.

Stefan inched slowly closer. "I have him, Uri. I have the president's son, and I'm taking him to the meeting place now."

"You must think me a fool!" Uri shouted.

"Let her go!" Logan roared.

"Logan," Maddie warned.

"Don't move, Mad Dog," Logan said, turning as Uri pulled Maddie backward, easing towards the shelter of the trees. He probably didn't even realize he was doing it. It was just natural instinct to seek cover.

"You will drop the gun," Uri growled into Maddie's ear.

"Do it, Mad Dog. It's OK."

"Logan ..."

Was Maddie's voice breaking? Was it all finally too much? Logan would rather be shot again than watch her shed a single tear.

"It's OK, Mad Dog. Just drop the gun. It'll be OK."

But the two Russians probably didn't hear a word of it. Stefan was inching closer and Logan didn't know who to fear. Who to trust. Except for Maddie. He had always trusted Maddie.

But no matter how you counted it, this new Russian was outnumbered. It was just a matter of time.

"It's gonna be OK," Logan said, knowing that Maddie

was more than capable of doing the math.

"I know it is," she said.

"I'm here," he told her, and watched her eyes go misty, because he *was* there. Logan was there and he was alive and he had carried her through a storm and bound her wounds.

He hadn't written her a single letter, but he hoped his actions would say so much more than words.

"You were careless, Stefan," Uri snapped. "You never should have let me live."

"I never meant to, I assure you," Stefan answered.

"What do you say, President's Son? Should I shoot the man who took you first? Or should I kill the girl he should have let me kill yesterday?"

"You don't need her!" Logan shouted, and Uri brought the gun to Maddie's temple.

"I know." Uri squeezed Maddie tighter. "Now drop your gun, little girl." There was no doubt he was out of patience. Especially when he shifted his aim and turned the barrel towards Logan. "Now."

"Logan?" Maddie said, the word a question: *Do you trust me? Will you forgive me? Will you still like me once you see who I really am?*

Logan shook his head, a warning. *DON'T TRY IT, MAD DOG*. But Maddie wasn't listening, so he shouted, "Take me!"

"Oh, I intend to." Then Uri spun. "Don't move, Stefan."

"I told you I was bringing them in," Stefan said.

Uri laughed. "If that was your intention, you would have let me kill the girl yesterday instead of shooting me like a coward. You still think you can save everyone, Stefan. But you can't save *anyone*."

Uri looked down at Maddie. "Isn't that right, sweetheart?"

"That's OK," Maddie said. "I'm kind of used to saving myself."

Maybe it was her words that knocked him off guard. Or maybe it was the way her skull crashed into his nose. But in any case Uri was pointing his gun in Maddie's direction in one moment and howling in pain the next.

Logan and Stefan watched, frozen, while she dropped to the icy ground and kicked at his legs, knocking him off balance.

The man was injured. Half starved and half frozen. But he was also half crazy with rage, and he came at her throat with both hands. Maddie didn't think. She just turned and rolled onto her back and pointed her gun straight up towards the canopy of trees.

And fired.

Logan and Maddie had been walking through the woods for hours, listening to the crack of trees under the weight of too much ice. The breaking limbs sounded like gunshots, Logan had thought at the time.

So it was almost surreal to hear the report of the pistol and then the sharp crack of the tree.

Uri was still over Maddie, strangling and screaming. He must have thought her a moron to waste a shot. But that would have been his last thought for a long time, because when the ice-covered tree limb landed atop him, he didn't move again.

"Maddie!" Logan screamed and ran towards her, but she was lost beneath the weight of the madman and the icy, heavy branch of the tree. Logan couldn't even see her. Nothing moved.

"Maddie, are you …? Maddie!"

"I'm fine. Just smushed."

At her muffled shout Logan didn't know whether to laugh or to scream.

And then he remembered Stefan.

Uri's gun must have come loose in the struggle or the crash because when Logan turned he found Stefan stooping down into the snow. The gun was in his hands.

And Logan knew it was too late.

For a second he stood frozen in the snow and the ice and the sun that had finally decided to start shining. He looked at the man who had knocked Maddie down a hill and dragged Logan towards some unknown fate – the man who had left two Secret Service agents dead in Maddie's cabin – and Logan had the sinking feeling that they were right back where they'd started.

But before he could lunge or strike out, Stefan tucked the gun into the waist of his jeans and looked at Logan.

"Let's get her out of there," he said.

"OK?" The word came out as a question, and Logan couldn't keep his gaze from slipping between Stefan and the gun.

"And then I'm going to tell you a story," Stefan said.

"A story about what?"

"A wolf."

Chapter 26

It had been a long time since Logan had had one of the nightmares. For years, though, they'd come to him in the dark: eyes better to see him with, teeth better to eat him with. The wolf had been there every time he'd closed his eyes. And whenever the world got too still or too quiet, he'd hear them again: the Russian words that he hadn't known the meaning to years ago, that he hadn't been able to forget ever since.

A boy is no match for a wolf.

He looked at Stefan. And a part of him wanted to growl.

But Maddie didn't have that problem.

"So …" She let the word draw out as she sat on a fallen log, legs crossed, like maybe she had just ordered a milkshake, like maybe this was the most ordinary thing in the world and she hadn't just hog-tied a rogue Russian to a tree. She actually took a moment to examine her nails. "Go ahead, Stefan. Tell us a story. Just make it a good one."

Behind her, Uri groaned, but Maddie must have had no doubts in her knot-tying ability because she didn't even turn around. She just kept staring up at the man who had tried to kill her, waiting as if they had all day.

"Six years ago, three men tried to take the first lady of the United States."

"We are aware," Maddie said. She gestured with her gun, a get-to-the-good-part gesture if Logan had ever seen one. But Stefan was deliberate as he talked on.

"You may think that is where the story begins, but in truth it started long before that day at the White House. Long before your father was the president. Long before any of us even existed. In a way, this all began more than eighty years ago, when a child was born in a Russian prison. Some say that he was kept there – in the prison, raised by two hundred mothers who were all criminally insane. But others swear that the guards did not want the responsibility of an infant, so they drew straws, and the loser took the baby to the woods – left him to be raised by the wolves."

"Stefan," Maddie said, "I really don't want to shoot you. But I will, you know. Right through the shoulder, make us nice and even."

But, to Stefan, it was like she hadn't spoken at all.

"My grandfather used to tell me stories from when he was a boy. In the coldest part of winter, he and his siblings would huddle in their beds, listen to the wolves howl, and wonder how one of the wolves could sound so human."

"The point, Stefan!" Maddie was up and stalking towards him. She was no longer laughing, not teasing. They were all cold and hungry and ready for the ordeal to be over, and Logan wondered if it might finally be impatience that got the best of her.

"They named him Boris, this boy, because, of course Boris means—"

"*Wolf*," Logan said.

"I know how it sounds. I know the stories are no doubt mostly myth, legend. But the man is real – of that much I am certain. And all legends are at least a little bit true. The people of my grandfather's village used to swear the child was feral, but he was also smart and ruthless. He was a boy when the war came. He was a young man as the Soviets rose, a man in his prime when they fell. He was born with nothing, but all it takes to rise to power is the willingness to do that which another will not."

Stefan paused and looked from Maddie to Logan, held his gaze.

"There was nothing the Wolf would not do. He had no family. No home. He was beholden only to his greed and his neverending quest for power. Until … Until he had a son."

Logan blinked and shook his head. The chill that ran down his spine had nothing to do with the cold.

"But the son wanted to be more than his father. More powerful. More wealthy. But, most of all, more feared. So he hatched a plan. He became obsessed with walking into the White House and taking the wife of the most powerful man in the world."

Logan remembered the man who had winked at him in the corridor, his tattoo and his words.

A boy is no match for a wolf.

"*Da*," Stefan said, and Logan realized he'd spoken aloud and in Russian.

"The plan was foolish, the risk not worth the reward. The Wolf knew that, and he forbade his son from taking such a stupid chance. But his son was full of bluster. And his son had a friend who was as arrogant and foolish as he was. So the two of them recruited another gun and ... you know the rest."

"So this is revenge?" Maddie, of course, had to cut right to the heart of the matter. "The Wolf lost his son, so he's going to take the president's son and call it even? Are we in old-school eye-for-an-eye territory? Is that it?"

"Yes. And no." Stefan was shaking his head, as if there were too many secrets in there and they were warring with each other, trying to get out. "The Wolf is sick. Dying. And without a son – an heir – he needs to make sure his legacy lives on." Stefan pointed at where Uri sat bound to the tree. "That man hoped to be his successor."

"And what are you?" Logan asked. "What was I, some kind of pawn? Some kind of test? Whoever brings me back first wins, is that it?"

"No. I'm the brother of the man who talked his son into defying him. So I must be made to suffer, too."

"Your sister," Maddie said, filling in the blank.

"She needs medicine. Without it, she will die, too. I had one chance to save her. All I had to do was bring the boy to the Wolf and I could have my sister and my family's debt would be erased." Stefan laughed the laugh of someone who doesn't find anything funny at all. "The best thugs in Russia, he has at his disposal, but he chooses me to do this thing because he wants to make as many people suffer as possible."

"You were supposed to take Logan to some meeting place, right? Will your sister be there? Or is she back in Russia?"

"She was supposed to be here. In Alaska. The Wolf is dying. He doesn't have much time. He will be there, too. He isn't going to wait for the boy to come to him. The Wolf will come to his prey."

A part of Logan wanted to laugh at Stefan, the words were so dramatic and surreal. But another part of Logan knew – a part had always known – that the Wolf was out there, howling in the night. And someday it was going to try to finish what was started six years ago.

"How?" Logan's voice was quiet as he turned back to Stefan. "How did Boris know I'd be in Alaska?"

Stefan almost smiled. "When you set up a secret social media account and post pictures about a big trip, you should remember that nothing in Russia stays a secret for long."

Logan looked at Maddie. He expected her to lecture

him, yell at him – at least call him an idiot. But she was up and moving towards the cliff almost before Logan could reach her.

"We need the pack," Maddie said.

"Wait."

"No!" she shouted. "We need to call my dad and get you out of here. Now that we know there aren't any moles in the Secret Service … We need to get help, Logan. Now."

But Logan was looking from the steep cliff to Stefan and then to Maddie, who had been knocked unconscious and shot and dragged into a fight that wasn't her own.

"How much time does your sister have?" he asked the man who might or might not still be their enemy.

Slowly Stefan shook his head. "Not enough."

Maddie's shoulder hurt. Her head throbbed. That was how she knew it was almost over. If there'd been no help on the horizon – no hope – her body would have blocked out those aches and pains. She would have found a way to go on.

But as soon as Maddie saw Logan slip over the edge of the ravine, she actually staggered and dropped to a fallen log. She should have been afraid, she guessed. Technically she was outnumbered.

But Uri, the fake ranger, was tied to a tree and

Maddie had a gun. But, most of all, Maddie had a new perspective on Stefan. He really wasn't a bad guy. But even good people can do bad things if given even just a little bit of a reason.

She saw him looking to the woods, to escape. So Maddie slipped the gun behind her back, tucking it into the waistband of her jeans. She saw him watch her do it.

"Don't run," she told him.

"Would you really shoot me?" He actually sounded like he might be teasing.

"Oh, I'd shoot you straight through the heart if I thought I had to. But I don't have to. And that's why you shouldn't run."

"They have my sister," he reminded her.

"And we're gonna call people who can get her back."

"Will they?" It wasn't a question. It was a dare. "Or will they take me to a place where I will never see the sun again? Maybe I will disappear forever."

"This isn't Russia," she reminded him, but Stefan's reply was a cold, hard laugh.

"Anywhere can be Russia. Besides, I took your prince."

"He's not *my* prince," Maddie snapped.

"He is American royalty. And I took him. I will never see freedom again. I will never see Natalia again. And I can live with that. *After* she is safe."

"If this Boris is as bad as you say he is—"

"He is worse," Stefan said, cutting her off.

"—then the Secret Service is going to want him. Trust me."

"She's very sick. Without her medicine …"

"They're already looking, I can promise you that. As soon as they realize their agents are dead, they'll—"

"They're not dead."

For a moment, Maddie was certain she'd misheard him. Maybe it was wishful thinking – hearing – on her part.

"What?"

"The men from the Secret Service … they are not dead. They were supposed to die, but I disabled them, tied them up inside your cabin. They are not dead."

Maddie hadn't realized how much that had weighed on her until the weight was lifted. She thought she might float away.

"They're alive."

"They were," Stefan said. "When I left them."

"Then help is coming," Maddie told him.

She got up and walked to the ledge, peered over. Logan looked so much bigger from that angle, all arms and legs, big strong hands that gripped the rocks. He'd reached the pack and he looked up, as if knowing that Maddie would be there. His smile was brighter than the sun.

"There's a rope!" he shouted.

"Throw it up!" she called back.

Five minutes later he was standing back at the top of the hill. He wasn't even breathing hard when he said, "We've got it."

Maddie thought she might cry. And maybe she would have if crying wasn't the world's leading cause of puffy eyes and skin blotchiness. For some reason, it seemed really, really important that Maddie's skin stay as blotch-free as possible in Logan's presence.

Logan dropped the pack to the ground and started digging through pockets.

"Food," he said with a sigh, tossing an energy bar in Maddie's direction. "Ibuprofen." He tossed the small bottle at her, too. "Take two of those. Now," he ordered. Maddie grinned, and for once in her life did as she was told.

"Where is it?" A hint of panic was seeping into Logan's voice. "Where is ...?"

But then his entire face changed. He took a deep breath, then pulled his hand from one of the pockets of the pack, the bright yellow phone gripped tightly in his hand.

"It's here."

Maddie thought she could kiss him.

She didn't, of course. But she could have. And it wasn't just out of relief or joy. It was because, in that moment, Logan just looked utterly kissable, and she didn't know what she thought about that.

"Give it," she ordered, and Logan handed it over. "Don't move!" she shouted as Stefan inched towards the trees.

Logan had already dropped the pack on a big, flat rock and was unloading it, carefully surveying exactly what they had.

There was the ibuprofen in a tiny white bottle. A canteen that was half full and three energy bars. A pack of Band-Aids, two empty plastic bags. A sleeping bag. A poncho. Two pairs of thick, tall socks, and something that looked like a solar phone charger.

Plus the map.

It was the most glorious collection of stuff that Maddie had ever seen. She ripped open the wrapper of the energy bar that Logan had handed her and then looked down at the satellite phone and dialed a number she knew by heart.

As it rang, she spread out the map and tried to locate their position, then pinpoint a place where her father could land.

They could meet up in an hour. Maybe significantly less. She was calling her father. Her father was coming. Maddie was so giddy she could practically hear the phone ringing on his end. She could practically …

She took another big bite of the energy bar, but then it suddenly turned to ashes in her mouth as she caught Logan's gaze.

"What's that noise?" he asked.

And Maddie realized that she wasn't imagining the sound of her father's phone ringing. She kept Stefan's sat phone to her ear, but she was no longer listening, not really.

She was looking at Logan, who was starting to rise, to turn, to look at the man who was now fully conscious, leaning against the tree, a cold, cruel smile across his face.

Maddie kept the phone to her ear, praying that she might hear her father say hello, or cuss, or cry. She wanted to hear her father's voice, but instead she heard his distinctive ringtone coming from the pocket of the ranger uniform.

She heard Uri ask, "Looking for someone?"

Maddie thought that maybe someone had knocked her off a cliff again. She felt like maybe, this time, she never would stop falling.

But Logan didn't have that problem.

"Where is it?" he shouted. He grabbed Uri by the lapels of his coat and pulled him as hard as he could with the man still tied to a tree. Logan started digging through pockets, ripping open the man's jacket until they both looked down at the ringing phone.

"Where did you get that?" Maddie's voice was cold and calm, but inside she was screaming. "Where did you get that?" she shouted this time, the words echoing out across the ice-cold river, maybe all the way to the sea.

But the man just smiled. "You didn't think the boy was all we wanted, did you?" He laughed like they were so silly. "The Wolf won't rest until he's hurt everyone who hurt his son. *Everyone*."

Maddie couldn't help but remember all the times she'd asked her father why they'd had to leave DC, what was so special about Alaska. She'd begged to go to school somewhere. She'd wanted to make friends. Even in the most remote parts of the world people had satellite Internet, but not Maddie. She'd thought it was because of what happened in that corridor in DC. She'd thought it was because her father had almost died.

But that wasn't it.

It was because her father had *lived*, and he must have known that someday soon the Wolf would be there, trying to huff and puff and blow their cabin down.

"Where is he?" Logan shook the man again, but Maddie was spinning on Stefan.

"Did you know?"

"No," Stefan said, shaking his head slowly, like maybe he'd been a fool not to. "But that is the way of the Wolf."

"Is my father alive?" she asked the man tied to the tree. "Is he?" she shouted, pulling the gun from her waistband and taking aim.

"Mad," Logan warned, but Maddie wasn't listening.

"Where is my father?" she asked again, the words almost a growl.

"He's safe. For now." There was an eerie glow in the Russian's eyes, like maybe it was worth being captured and shot and knocked unconscious by an icy limb just to have such a good seat for her heartbreak.

"They'll keep him alive. He might even save himself, you know."

"How?" Logan asked.

The Russian smiled up at him. "By killing you, of

course. The Wolf has always liked a trade. Maybe if he kills you, the Wolf will spare him. It's only a pity we did not know about the girl. We were told the daughter died in DC. The Wolf will be most distressed to learn he was mistaken."

"Don't look at her!" Logan shouted. His hands were around the man's throat. "You don't get to look at her or speak to her. You aren't good enough to breathe the same air as her, you—"

"Logan," Maddie tried.

"I will end you," Logan told the man.

"Logan," Maddie tried again, this time grabbing his hand. "They have my dad."

"I know, Mad Dog. We're going to get him back. We're—"

"Not we." She was shaking her head. She should have been screaming or crying, but her heart was numb, from the worry and the cold. For the first time in a long time she could see things plainly. It was like hunting, being all alone in the early hours of the day when everything is quiet and still and covered in freshly fallen snow. At times like that you can see farther, hear more. The world was crystal clear in that moment, and Maddie knew exactly what had to happen.

"You've got to call DC, Logan. You have to tell the Secret Service where you are. Tell them where my dad is. Tell them—"

"OK, Mad Dog. We will. We'll tell them. And then—"

"No." Maddie was shaking her head. She eased farther away from the Russians, and Logan followed. It was as if both of them knew that this moment was too personal, too raw and too real to be shared with strangers.

Logan's arms went around her, sheltering her between his body and the low branch of a tree, gripping the cold wood despite the ice and the snow. Maddie laid her forehead against Logan's broad chest, resting for what felt like the first time. And the last.

"Mad Dog." Logan's voice was as soft as his touch as he lifted her chin, then gently tucked a piece of hair behind her ear. It said a lot about her situation that she no longer cared what her hair looked like. Or her skin. She only cared that she finally knew why her father had brought her to this big, empty world – why he'd kept her safe and taught her to survive here.

Because someday, she was going to have to return the favor.

"Tell me you know the phone number."

"Of course I know the phone number." Logan sounded more than a little bit offended.

"Tell me you'll call them."

"Mad Dog, of course I'm going to call them."

She put her hand over his. "Tell me you know where we are right now – that you know what to tell them. They have to send a chopper here. Now."

"Yes, Maddie. I know. But—"

There was a click, the sound faint but sharp in the cold

air. For a moment Logan froze until Maddie went up on her toes and pressed her mouth to his for one split second.

"Tell me you forgive me."

But Maddie didn't wait for Logan's answer as he stared down at the shiny metal that hung around his wrist. He moved to reach for her, but the limb of the tree shook, showering them with falling snow. Logan tried again, then cursed, and Maddie had to mentally alter her list of supplies. They had:

Ibuprofen.

Socks.

Poncho.

Sleeping bag.

Solar charger.

Band-Aids.

And handcuffs. Maddie hadn't dared to forget about the handcuffs.

"Mad Dog," Logan started. "What did you—"

"Call them." She dropped Stefan's yellow phone a few feet away from Logan, where he could reach it with a little effort. "As soon as we're gone. Get them here. Save yourself."

"Maddie, wait!" Logan lunged for her but the cuff held tight.

"You're the president's son! If something happens to you, there could be war, Logan. Straight up war. The stock market could crash. There'd be congressional investigations and ... I always really liked your mom.

She's got to be worried sick. So call her. And let me do what I have to do."

"Not without me."

But something had happened inside of Maddie the moment she heard the sound of her father's phone. It was like she was above the Arctic Circle and the sun had gone down and she was standing on the front end of a long, dark winter.

"You seem to think this is a democracy, Logan. It's not. It's Alaska."

She knew that Logan kept shouting, cursing, but he might as well have been yelling at the snow because Maddie was already turning to Stefan.

"You know where they are?" she asked.

"I do."

"Will my father be where your sister is?"

"Probably."

"And the Wolf? Will he be there?"

"Definitely," Stefan said. "The Wolf has waited six long years for this moment. He will be where the blood is."

Maddie walked to the pack and gathered everything that she might need.

"Then let's go kill him."

Chapter 27

"What's she like?"

Maddie didn't turn back to look at Stefan, but she knew that he was back there. She could hear his heavy breath and his footsteps crunching in the icy snow. But most of all, she knew that he had just as much reason to fight as she did. She was just glad that they were finally fighting on the same side.

"Natalia?" he said.

"Yes. How long have they had her?"

This time, it took a moment for Stefan to answer. Maybe because time didn't have any meaning anymore, with the short Alaskan days and gloomy, sunless sky. But more than likely because it felt like forever to Stefan. It was a feeling Maddie could relate to.

"Four days. The Wolf came for her four days ago."

Just four days. It wasn't much time, but it was forever in a lot of ways. Maddie knew better than anyone that it only took a moment for a life to change forever.

"What happens if she doesn't get her medicine?"

"It depends," Stefan said. "She is diabetic. She needs a daily shot of insulin. Depending on what she's been eating – *if* she's been eating … I do not know. She will likely need a doctor. The Wolf promised he would bring one. He was supposed to bring one. But the Wolf … he lies."

"She'll be fine," Maddie told him. "We're going to get her back."

The air was slightly warmer and the ground was covered with a slick sheen of water. Maddie hadn't known that there could be anything slicker than ice, but that was before she'd moved to Alaska. Now she knew that the ground could always be slicker, rougher, steeper. Things could always get worse. And they usually did before they got better.

She stopped for a moment when they reached the top of the ridge. Down below, there was an icy lake and a silt-covered beach. A familiar red plane floated in the distance, and it was all Maddie could do not to scream out for her father and run in its direction. She would have, too, if it hadn't been for the helicopter not far away. And the tents.

"That's it?" Maddie said – the words a question. Somehow, she'd expected something far bigger, darker, scarier. They'd been walking for more than a day, every step bringing them closer to this place. In a way, Maddie realized, this was where that White House corridor led.

Six years later, she was finally going to come out the other side.

"Binoculars," Maddie said, holding out her hands. Stefan gave her the pair they'd scavenged from the fake ranger's gear, and Maddie laid low on the ground. The snow and ice didn't melt through her raincoat, but she could feel it on her legs. It didn't matter. She trained the binoculars on the camp below, memorizing every possible detail.

"I count four guards," she said, handing the binoculars to Stefan. "Does that sound right to you?"

He looked into the binoculars and scanned the camp. "Yes. The Wolf would never leave home with fewer than two. Two extras make sense under the circumstances."

Smoke rose from a big fire that someone had built between the two tents. Three of the armed guards were positioned on the perimeter, scanning the trees. Waiting. For Stefan or Uri. For trouble.

Maddie looked up at the overcast sky.

"What is it?" Stefan asked her.

"There has to be a satellite looking for Logan. Drones, too. Someone's going to see that fire and come asking questions."

"Isn't that a good thing?"

"Yeah," Maddie admitted. "I think so. Logan will have called in the cavalry by now. Help could be just over that ridge."

Stefan looked at her. "Or not."

Maddie nodded. "Or not."

"So what do we do now?" Stefan was actually asking. She wasn't some tagalong, some annoying girl. She was the person with home advantage, and he was smart enough to see it. She liked him for it. Even if she also still kind of hated him for trying to kill her and messing up her hair and all.

Maddie pushed up onto her knees in the snow. She started to stand.

It took her a moment to register that Stefan was standing behind her, and Uri's gun was in his hand. Maybe it was the way the sun was getting lower, the sky darker, but everything seemed to change as the ice bled through the denim of Maddie's jeans and the world got very dark and very cold.

"Uri was right, you know. You are the only child of the man who took the Wolf's only child." Stefan stared down the sight of the gun. "You would be more than enough to trade for my sister."

Logan was going to kill Maddie. As soon as he was certain she was safe, of course.

The metal cuff felt tighter, colder, when she was the one to put it on him, so he pulled against the limb again and growled and cursed under his breath.

Only the sound of the laughter made him stop.

"Your woman is either very smart. Or very stupid," the Russian said.

"Don't kid yourself, comrade," Logan told him. "She's both."

The yellow sat phone was lying in the snow. Waterproof, freeze-proof … idiot-proof. He just had to reach it. He just had to stretch. Sinking down, Logan stuck out one of his too-long legs, finally grateful for the extra inches as he eased the phone close enough to grab.

"They will kill him, you know," Uri said as if they were just making conversation. As if Logan actually cared about his opinion.

"Your new friend Stefan. The Wolf will shoot him dead." For some reason, when the silence came, Logan had to look at the man. He saw the look in Uri's eyes when he said, "The girl will not be so lucky."

Logan lunged for the man, but the cuff held and jerked him back, shaking snow and ice from the tree, raining down on top of him like fire.

"And you wonder why she left you," the man said with a laugh.

Logan turned back to the tree, looking at the icy branches, calculating the weight of the snow and the circumference of the limb. Then he started to climb, carefully, balancing himself on the icy length, edging farther and farther from the base of the tree until the limb snapped, crashing into the snow and taking Logan with it.

"Nicely done," the Russian mocked. "You're smarter

than a tree. Your father must be so proud."

Logan's father was probably worried sick. For the first time, Logan let himself admit that much. The most powerful man in the world was probably frozen with grief. Logan couldn't even think about what his mother was probably feeling.

And Maddie ...

Would they have reached the camp yet? Would she have seen her father?

How many rounds of ammo were there in the two guns? And did she get her other knife back – the little one that Stefan had taken? Maddie wasn't the kind of girl to be content with just one knife, after all.

But most of all, Logan wanted to know that she was going to be OK.

"They probably aren't dead yet," Uri told him. "If you leave now, you can catch them. Stop them."

"Stop them from what?"

"Walking into a trap."

"Those are big words for a man who got knocked unconscious and tied to a tree by a teenage girl," Logan reminded him.

"The girl's going to die, President's Son. And so is your new friend Stefan. If he thought the Wolf would honor his bargain, he is a fool. The Wolf lost everything six years ago. And before he dies, he is going to take all of his enemies down with him."

Logan was on his feet. He was reaching for the phone

and wiping away the snow that covered the keys. It was cold in his hand, but it felt like life itself as he looked down at the screen and began to dial a number he knew by heart.

When he heard the beeping he thought it might have been the phone finding a signal, maybe it was the White House switchboard, connecting him to a line.

But then Logan pulled the phone from his ear and looked down at the little flashing battery. When the screen went blank it felt like the part of him that had faith, that believed deep down that everything might be OK, turned off, too.

For a long time, he just stood, staring at the blank screen. The battery wasn't low. It was dead. The phone was a useless weight in his hands. And suddenly it was all too much.

He roared and almost threw it off the cliff, into the icy river below, before he remembered the charger.

Logan raced to the big, flat rock where the remnants of the packs were laid out. Maddie and Stefan must have taken Maddie's father's phone, so Logan grabbed Stefan's solar phone charger like it was a lifeline in a stormy sea. But the sky was so overcast that the phone didn't even register a charge. Not yet.

Logan looked around the big, flat rock at their collection of gear, but the map was gone, and Logan swore again to kill Maddie Manchester. Just as soon as he got her back.

"Having trouble?" Uri asked. Logan didn't think twice, lunging towards him.

"Where did they go?" he yelled.

But Uri shrugged, indifferent. "To their deaths, of course."

The map was still locked away in Logan's memory – locked inside his mind. But he didn't trust his bearings. There was too much at stake and the light was getting too low, and Logan knew that if he got turned around – if he missed a single landmark – he might never make it in time.

Logan grabbed the man and shook him, pounding his head into the tree. "Tell me where the camp is," he growled out.

"Why?" the Russian asked. "If I tell you where to find the girl, you're going to do what? Save the day? Let me go? Or maybe you will just kill me if I refuse."

"No." Logan let go and backed off. Angry as he was, he wasn't a killer. "You can either take me to the camp or stay here, tied to that tree, and wait for the bears to get hungry. It's your call."

Chapter 28

Maddie's hands were starting to tingle. Maybe it was nerves. Or the cold. Or maybe it was just what happened when you had to walk down a mountain and across a wide, snow-covered beach towards a wolf, all while keeping your hands on top of your head. All without trying to look back at the man who had the gun pointed directly at your spine.

She felt silly, really, in spite of everything. Sure, Stefan was taller and stronger and older. And he had a gun. But Maddie should have been able to take him. She would have been embarrassed if this ever got back to her friends.

But that was the upside to not having friends, Maddie realized. There wasn't a soul around to judge her, so Maddie walked on.

"Don't stop."

Stefan poked her in the back with the gun, pushing her slightly. She stumbled a little. Holding her hands that way made her shoulder ache and messed with her balance, but she absolutely refused to fall.

Stefan spoke again, but this time the words were in Russian and under his breath.

Logan could have interpreted, if he'd been there. But he wasn't. Logan was safe on the other side of the mountain. The Secret Service might have even found him already. She liked the thought of him in a helicopter with a heavy blanket over his shoulders, a hot drink in his hands.

Maddie would have given anything for a hot drink. But it was enough for her, the idea that maybe one of them might have already made it out of this ordeal alive.

Her arms dropped a little, fatigue settling in.

"Keep them up!" Stefan shouted with another push at her back. She took two large steps, stumbling forward and struggling to right herself.

And that was when she saw them.

The men appeared on the edges of her vision, assault rifles in their hands.

Stefan leveled his gun at her, but she stopped, looked back.

Something like pride glistened in his eyes as he said, "Tell the Wolf I've brought him something."

Not *someone*, Maddie realized. She was a *thing*, a piece of leverage.

One of the men laughed and the other joined in. When the second man spoke, it was in Russian, but Stefan sneered at the words. Then he answered, in English.

"She's better than the boy. Trust me. The Wolf will want to see this for himself."

The two guards must have been convinced because they gestured them towards the center of the camp.

"My sister?" Stefan asked.

One of the men nodded. "Alive" was his reply.

The two men fell into step on either side of Stefan. They kept their rifles pointed at the ground, but ready. Like one gunman might not be enough against a teenage girl. Maddie might have smiled, told herself that her reputation preceded her, but her shoulder hurt and her stomach growled. And she really had to go to the bathroom.

When they neared the tents, there was a rustling, and a moment later a man was standing before them, silhouetted by the smoke.

He was taller than she'd thought he'd be. Younger. Stronger. But when Maddie was finally close enough to see his eyes, she knew the mistake she'd just made.

"Where's the Wolf?" Stefan snapped at the man.

"Behind you," came a voice.

Slowly, Maddie turned. And she knew. It wasn't just that he was older. No. His eyes were cold and gray, but there was a fire inside of them. With one glance, Maddie feared she might get burned. They were the eyes of an animal, one dangerous and trapped. And right then Maddie understood the rumors and the nickname. She could believe that this man had been abandoned in a forest and raised by the wolves. He wasn't a man. He was a feral beast, and Maddie shivered a little in spite of herself.

For a moment, she stood in the cold wind, hands fisted overhead, letting the man look his fill. Then he glanced at one of the guards. "Take his sister to the woods and shoot her."

The man turned for one of the tents, but Stefan was lunging forward.

"No! Wait!"

"We had a deal, Stefan," the Wolf told him. "Your sister for the boy. This is no boy."

"She's better," Stefan shouted, but the Wolf spun. It was like no one had dared to raise their voice to him in sixty years. And no one had, Maddie was certain.

"Kill him, too," the Wolf told the gunmen.

Stefan raised his gun, but he was too slow. The butt of an assault rifle was already slicing through the air, clipping him on the back of the head.

He went down hard and Maddie jerked free. She dropped her arms and started to run, but the second guard had already taken hold of her. He spat something in Russian, and the Wolf looked her over once again.

"Kill them all."

He turned and started towards the tent like he hadn't just ordered the deaths of three people. Like this was just another day, and nothing could surprise him – not anymore.

Well … nothing except the small, female voice behind

him, saying, "Well, that would just be silly."

When the Wolf turned back to Maddie, it was like he was surprised she could speak. Or at the very least, that she didn't have the good sense to sound terrified. But she didn't. If anything, she sounded … bored.

"You need better sources, Mr Wolf Man," she told the most dangerous man in Russia.

"Why is that?" he asked her, honestly curious.

Maddie looked up at the cloudy sky then back to him, like she had all the time in the world.

"Well, because, (A) the Secret Service agent you've been obsessed with for six years doesn't have a *dead* daughter. He has an *awesome* daughter. And (B) I'm more than a little offended you didn't recognize the grade A hostage material that you have in front of you. I mean, if you're in the vengeance business I am a way better catch than Logan, who is an idiot, by the way."

"And C?" The Wolf almost smiled.

Behind him, Maddie could see a guard dragging a girl from one of the tents. She was weak and filthy, her face puffy with too many tears. But she was still alive and that was all that mattered.

"Stefan!" the girl shouted, but her voice was weak.

"C is easy, Boris." The Wolf turned back to Maddie, clearly confused by her smile. "You should have never let me get this close."

When Maddie pulled back her fist, the men didn't lunge, they didn't stop her. *How hard can she hit?* they all seemed to think in unison, but Maddie wasn't swinging at them. Instead, she was spinning, arm swirling through the air until she opened her fist and gray dust hurled towards the flames.

Stefan was diving towards his sister, tucking her into his arms and rolling away.

Maddie saw it, knew the girl was safe.

It was her last thought before the world caught fire.

Chapter 29

As soon as Logan heard the explosion, he stopped running and ducked instinctively as the flames formed a pillar that looked like it might be holding up the sky. For a split second, bright light overpowered the dusk. Dark smoke followed, billowing upward and blocking out the sun that was setting on the cloud-filled horizon.

The whole world turned black in that instant, and when it cleared, absolutely no one was still standing.

That was the bad news.

But the good news was that any disaster that large could only mean one thing: Maddie was still alive.

Maddie was an idiot. Or so she thought as she forced herself up and away from the fire that still roared behind her.

She'd shaved the entire block of magnesium, kept it clutched in her hands. Even though she knew it burned at four thousand degrees – even though that was exactly why she'd done it – she was still afraid her skin might blister, her hair might catch fire. She'd jumped as far from the flames as possible, and then all she had to do was roll and kick and claw her way over the body of the man who had fallen beside her.

One of the men with the assault rifles.

Maddie didn't think twice before picking up the weapon.

Through the smoke, Stefan stirred.

"The plane!" Maddie shouted. "Get to the plane. Now!"

Stefan didn't have to be told twice. He stood and swooped his frail little sister into his arms and started running to where her father's plane bobbed near the shore.

But Maddie couldn't leave yet. She would never leave without her father.

She crawled to the second gunman. Blood streamed from his head and he didn't move, so she grabbed his rifle and hurled it with all her might, sending it end over end into the icy water like she might be returning it to the Lady of the Lake.

Both of the men by the fire were unconscious, but Maddie knew there were two more guards out in the woods.

Two guards who would have no doubt heard the explosion.

Two guards who would be coming. Soon.

She forced herself to her feet. She was still wobbly,

but there was no time to worry about a pesky little thing like balance, so she rushed towards the tent, hurled back the flap, and yelled, "Dad?"

It was empty.

Maddie felt her legs start to give out. She was more tired, more hungry, more hopeless than she'd ever been in her life.

But then she turned and saw her father—

—on his knees in the snow, the Wolf's blade at his neck.

Maddie had left Logan the little knife. He thought he might have to thank her for that when this mess was over. Right after he killed her. Then kissed her. Then killed her again.

But the knife did come in handy. So did the rope.

Uri had struggled as Logan led him through the forest, but the man had stayed on his feet long enough to guide Logan to the camp. When the time came to tie Uri to another tree, the man's wound had started to fester and the fight was leaving him bit by bit. He didn't even try to struggle. He only smirked.

"Thanks for the tour," Logan said. He crammed one of Stefan's spare socks into the man's mouth. "I think I can find my way from here."

From that point, it was just a matter of waiting.

Of course, it didn't take long for Uri to spit out the gag. Of course, he started yelling. Even his grunts sounded Russian as they filled the woods.

And when the perimeter guard recognized Uri, the man rushed right towards him.

It was easier than Logan thought to pull back the tree branch he'd leveraged, send it hurling right towards the guard, and knock him off his feet. Then Logan pounced, pulling back his fist the way Maddie's dad had once taught him.

"You never know when you might meet a bully," Mr Manchester had said.

It was a lesson Logan would never, ever forget.

The Wolf really was dying. It wasn't just the pallor of his skin, the way his clothes hung on his frame like he used to be a much larger man. It was also the desperation that seemed to be seeping from his pores. He was going to get his revenge. Even if it killed him.

Especially if it killed him. But that suited Maddie just fine.

"Drop the knife," she told him.

The assault rifle was heavy in her hands. She'd never touched one before. The only thing a gun like this hunted was people, and Maddie felt a little sick just holding it. But she didn't dare let it go.

The Wolf didn't care, though. He just laughed and brought the knife closer to her father's throat. A small drop of blood appeared on the edge of the blade, but her father didn't even wince.

His eyes were black and his lip was swollen, but he sounded exactly like himself when he ordered, "Get out of here, Mad."

"But, *Dad*—" Maddie drew out the word. "I just got here. You never let me have any fun."

"You were dead," the Wolf said. He almost sounded impressed. Then he tightened his grip on the knife. "And soon you will be again."

But before he could pierce her father's skin further, Maddie's dad threw back his head, catching Boris on the chin and knocking him off balance.

Her dad's hands were bound, but he moved like that was his preferred way of fighting as he threw himself at the old man, knocking him to the icy ground.

He was rising, leveraging himself over the Wolf when a shot rang out from the distance, and Maddie's father collapsed, blood spreading across his back.

"Maddie!" Logan's shout echoed across the lake, and Maddie spun. Froze. Because there he was, racing towards her.

He was supposed to be safe and warm and halfway through his sixth bowl of soup by now. He was supposed to have sent the Secret Service. He was supposed to have forgotten all about Maddie. Again. But he hadn't, and she honestly didn't know whether she should love him or hate him for it.

Boris was righting himself, pushing aside the limp form of Maddie's father, and Maddie saw the look in his eyes as he realized that the first son was walking willingly into camp, his hands over his head.

"Take me!" Logan shouted.

Another shot rang out, ricocheting off one of the big, flat rocks near the water. Then Boris shouted something in Russian and the firing stopped.

And Logan walked on, like this was the moment he'd been waiting for. Like this was the most important moment in his life. And maybe the last.

"I know who you are," Logan said. He kept his gaze locked on the old man. "You're the great Wolf. Your son came to start a war. He died a soldier's death. This man shot him." Logan pointed to where Maddie's father lay on the ground. "Because it was his *job* to protect *me*. It was always about me. My father. My mother. It was about my family then. It should be about my family now. So take me."

"I intend to," the Wolf said.

"But let the soldier and the girl go. One son for one son," Logan said, and for a moment it looked like the Wolf might laugh. Then Logan said, "Let them live to tell your story. Let them turn you into a legend – not just in Russia, but all over the world."

This, at last, seemed to make the old man wonder.

Maddie was aware of the guards pulling themselves upright, coming towards her. One of them gripped her too tight by the arm, shook her a little just to prove he was a big, tough guy as he ripped the rifle out of her hands.

But the Wolf said something in Russian and the man's grip loosened. Then he let go completely and forced her towards her father with a shove.

"Tell them," the Wolf said. "Go tell the world how the first son died."

Maddie looked at where her father lay on the ground, bleeding. Then to Logan, who had dropped to his knees. The Wolf strode towards him with purpose. It was almost ceremonial, almost sacred.

Logan wasn't the first son. He was a sacrificial lamb as he knelt at the old man's feet.

"Logan," Maddie warned, but he just smiled at her.

"Dear Mad Dog," he said softly. "I'm sorry I didn't write back sooner. But that doesn't mean I didn't miss you. I missed you every single day. Love, Logan."

"No!" Maddie's scream pierced the air, but the Wolf was already bringing his blade to Logan's throat.

"A son for a son," the Wolf said. He pulled back the blade.

Then stumbled. Staggered.

When he glanced down at his chest he seemed more confused than in pain. He looked from the knife in his own hand to the blade that was stuck hilt-deep in his chest, right where his heart would have been if he'd had one.

The old man seemed so confused as he dropped to the

ground beside Logan.

Then he looked at the girl.

Her arm was still outstretched. Follow-through was everything, after all. And even she hadn't been vain enough to bedazzle both her favorite hatchet *and* her favorite throwing knife.

Her aim had been dead on.

For a moment, the only sound was the crackling fire. The hired guns didn't move, like they had no idea how to live in a world without the Wolf.

Then a soft voice said, "Mad Dog?" Her father stirred. The trance ended. And the Russians seemed to realize where they were and who they'd almost killed.

The two of them came then, rage and fear seeping out of them. The man with the rifle raised it, preparing to shoot. Just as the shot rang, Maddie dived, sliding across the snow and ice, reaching for her father.

She braced for the impact of the bullet, the stinging and the burn, but it was the Wolf's guard who was falling. His rifle dropped useless to the snowy ground, and Maddie looked back to see Stefan running from the woods, another rifle in his arms.

"Guess Stefan found the fourth guard," Logan said.

The other man had picked up the Wolf's knife, though, and he brandished it like a sword.

"Drop it," Maddie told him.

"You are unarmed. And a girl."

"She's the girl who killed the Wolf," Logan told the

man. "And she's not alone."

Maddie smiled. It was sweet. She felt almost sorry for calling him an idiot. But then she realized what he'd said and that it was true. She *wasn't* alone. For the first time in six years she didn't have to rely almost entirely on herself. She had her father back, and Stefan. And Logan.

Maddie didn't let herself wonder how long it would last. It was enough that it was true for now.

Then Logan looked up at the overcast sky, and Maddie realized the full depth of his words. Helicopters filled the dim horizon like a flock of birds. The sun was almost down, and soon ice and snow and glacier silt would be swirling in the air, blinding them.

Maddie threw her body over her father, but he pushed her aside, smoothed her hair. "I'm OK, Mad Dog. I've had worse."

And those were the words that finally broke her.

Tears streamed down her face and she cried in awful, eye-puffing, skin-blotching, gut-wrenching sobs.

"I've got you, Mad Dog. You're OK."

But was she OK?

She couldn't help herself. She looked at Logan.

"Uri and another guard are tied up in the woods," he reported.

"I left a man unconscious on that ridge," Stefan said, pointing in the direction from which he'd appeared.

"Where's your sister?" she asked.

"In the plane," he said, then looked longingly at it.

“Can you fly?” she asked him.

“A bit,” he said.

“Then go.” Maddie didn’t stop and think about the words, what they meant or how far the aftermath might follow them. She just knew that he’d been there for them in the end, and he was right. He’d taken the closest thing the US had to royalty. He might never see the sun.

“Get in the plane and leave. Now. Float it out around the bend and then take off as soon as you’re out of sight of the choppers. Fly as low as you can, and we’ll cover for you, but you have to get out of here. Now. Get your sister to a doctor and then go to ground and stay there. Both of you.”

“Maddie …” Logan started, and she spun on him.

“Right?” she asked.

Logan put the yellow sat phone and its charger in Stefan’s hand. “We’ll call you when the coast is clear.”

“Dad?” Maddie asked.

“Do it” was all her father said.

Then Stefan was running through the snow, and the plane was roaring to life and floating away while the helicopters looked like hornets on the horizon.

But Maddie stayed on the icy ground, holding tight to her father.

“The Wolf’s dead, Dad. It’s over. I think it’s really over.”

He looked up at her. “I’m sorry I never told you. I didn’t want to scare you. You were just a kid and you’d been through too much. I'm sorry."

"Shh. Save your strength. Help's coming. We're going to get you well and then go home."

Home.

It wasn't until the helicopters landed and two dozen agents in full SWAT gear swarmed the beach that Maddie realized she actually wasn't sure where that was anymore.

Chapter 30

FROM THE DESK OF MADELEINE ROSE MANCHESTER

To whom it may concern,

I don't know what brought you to this little shed, but I hope you'll be happy here – for however long you need to stay. I've taken the liberty of restocking the woodpile and bringing some new blankets and a few dishes, some matches and a mirror (because even though you may be the only person for twenty miles in any direction, most people feel better when they know what their hair looks like).

Help yourself to the canned goods – that's what they're here for.

But, most of all, be careful and take care of this place. It's special to me.

Maddie

(and me, too – Logan)

It was the first week of January, which, in Maddie's experience, meant five layers. So no wonder she couldn't help but feel incredibly underdressed. Her skirt was too short. Her tights were too thin. Her shoes weren't even waterproof, and no matter how many strongly worded emails Maddie had written in protest, she had been strictly warned to leave her hatchet and both of her knives at home.

So Maddie was basically naked, in other words, as she stood outside the tall fence, looking at the wilderness that lay on the other side of the electric gates.

It was unknown terrain filled with potential predators, and Maddie didn't like the look of it one bit.

"I can't do this," she said, pulling back. But she didn't go far before there was an arm around her waist, holding her firmly against a body that, if possible, had gotten even taller.

Logan looked down at her.

"Of course you can. You're Maddie Freaking Manchester. You caught a Russian kidnapper with a bear trap and a tree."

"Technically, I caught one Russian with a tree. I only wounded the second Russian with a bear trap."

"See? You're a natural. You're gonna fit right in."

"No." Maddie pulled back, tugging Logan's arm and trying her best to keep him in place when he started for the entry. "I can't do it. I don't belong here."

"Your dad needs surgery, Mad Dog. And physical

therapy. And to sit through about a million debriefs. When that's all done, you can go back. I promise. But in the meantime you can't stay in Alaska by yourself. So please, stay here. With me? Please."

It all sounded so great in theory, but there was traffic on the street – cars and trucks whizzing by so fast that Maddie felt a little dizzy. The sidewalks were filled with people who never looked up from their phones, all of them seemingly in the middle of nowhere. But they weren't.

Maddie knew what the middle of nowhere looked like, felt like. It didn't smell like bus exhaust and it didn't taste like a breakfast that came from a bag.

Maddie's fingers itched and she wanted to run, but all she could say was "Logan, I don't go to school. I do worksheets and read library books and chop wood all winter. Seriously. If anyone in there needs some wood chopped or a generator repaired, then I'm their girl, but—"

"Mad Dog."

Logan cupped her cheeks with his big, warm hands, made her look up into his eyes.

"You're *my* girl," he said, and then he kissed her, right there in front of their school and his Secret Service detail – right in front of the world. So she kissed him back again.

And again.

And again.

Until he pulled back and looked into her eyes. "If anything goes wrong in there, I'll save you."

She took his hand. "Not if I save you first."

Acknowledgments

In many ways, this is the most research-heavy book that I've ever written, because, in many ways, it's also the most realistic. Always before, I've written in worlds largely of my own making, but Alaska is a very real, very vast, very fascinating place, and I felt the need to get it as right as possible.

To that end, I went where people should always go for reliable answers: to librarians!

So I'd like to offer my most heartfelt thanks to Ida Olson, Elizabeth M. Nicolai and Andrea Hirsh for their help in understanding life and survival in rural Alaska.

I'd also like to thank "Klondike Kevin," the guide who showed my family around Skagway and told us that the groundwater could kill us, thus making me desperate to set a book there.

Finally, I have to thank Kristin Nelson, David Levithan, and the wonderful team at Scholastic as well as all the amazing authors I harassed for a solid six months to try to get the title just right. I owe you, each and every one!

About the Author

Ally Carter is the *New York Times* bestselling author of the Embassy Row series, as well as the Gallagher Girls and Heist Society series. Her books have been published all over the world, in over twenty languages. You can visit her online at www.allycarter.com.